Nudist Among Us

by
Allen Parker

PublishAmerica
Baltimore

First printing

ISBN: 1-4137-0178-7
PUBLISHED BY PUBLISHAMERICA, LLLP
www.publishamerica.com
Baltimore

Printed in the United States of America

An Introduction and Explanation

Most books are of a specific style. They are either short stories, or poems, or perhaps a riveting novel. This book is not. I am not the sort of person who stands on tradition, but I do have a tendency to apologize for my informality. I enjoy the variety of life, the unusual, and the strange. It is from this point that I bring you this, my inner thoughts.

I have written this collection of stories, poems, and letters as a literary way of expressing my thoughts. Some will make you laugh, God willing, others will make you think, and the rest is just so much about nothing. What I do want to accomplish is to express my feelings as a Christian, first, and to allow others to get some joy out of this. If you find this a little confusing at first, it will pass. If you find it enjoyable at first, it may pass, also. "You pays your money, and you takes your chances."

One suggestion I have for you is to sink yourself into reading. Not just this book, but any literary item. Find a character that reads the book for you. Don't just be your boring own self; really experience the story from another perspective. I find that being someone else while reading gives me a completely new and exciting look into that author's work.

In high school, I was forced to read *Death of a Salesman,* a story line that I found particularly not funny or interesting. I, however, enjoyed reading it later when my John, the Axe Murderer, character read it. The story changed a little; I'm not sure that Mr. Miller ever considered having Biff bludgeoned a few times, but I completed the *Death of a Salesman* within the allotted time with sufficient knowledge retained. You might want to be a Church Treasurer in the "Letter to Finance Committee." You could be a pastor while reading "Nudist Among Us." I personally liked being the milk man while rereading the "Paper Boy." Don't let me influence you, though. Be whatever you want to be.

No person is a self-made man. We develop with the influences and help from others. The love and hate that we experience every day builds us into the people we are. Without the help of several people, I could not have assembled this book. I feel compelled to mention just a few of them out of a sense of fairness. I do regret not having enough space to acknowledge everyone.

First, there is my wife, a lady who has put up with me for many years, thinks that I am not as funny as I think I am, but has never ceased to love me anyway. There is also my son, who still thinks that I am the funniest man around, even at the ripe old age of twelve. I thank my parents who have supported my writing for many years. I also must thank Matthew Koval who's editing help was invaluable.

One person that I must also mention is my sister, who made me so jealous of her musical ability that I learned to laugh every time someone mentioned her success. Before anyone asks, this book is not about getting her back for the mountains of times that she has waved success in front of me. I have not exaggerated about her, either. She really does have green hair, a crooked nose, and a big hump on her back.

Last, but certainly not least, are the dear friends that have stuck beside me and laughed at my jokes, even the funny ones. Friends cost less than a dime a dozen, but are worth more that their weight in gold.

Paper Boy

My first introduction to nudism was at the impressionable age of fourteen. My parents, sister and I lived in a small Virginia town. We lived in a neighborhood not far from the school and close to our church. The neighborhood was bustling with boys and girls my age playing in the streets constantly. There was never a shortage of ways to get into trouble.

Down the block and at the end of the road was an old house that resembled the rustic, old, mountain lodge that my grandfather kept for a hunting lodge. I always thought it cool that my grandfather had a hunting lodge. He and his old army buddies would head up to the mountains every year for the first week of hunting season. They would stay up there and live off of the land, playing cards and retelling the same old stories. When they returned home smelly and unshaved, they would slap each other on the back and say, “See ya next year.”

Being a teenager and especially fond of hunting, I longed to be included in these trips. Sure of my hunting skills and tracking ability, I thought that I would be an asset to these guys’ hunting adventure. But that was the year that I learned that none of them ever carried a gun with them. I guess they just hung out at the cabin and waited for the deer to knock on the door and surrender. It wasn’t too many years later that Grandma put her foot down and forced Grandad to sell the place. I think that was the year that she found out that the National Forest they were supposed to be hunting in had been closed to hunting for several years. That was the last hunting trip. But I digress.

The summer ushered in my fourteenth birthday and my first contact with nudists. I wouldn't realize it for another fifteen years, but the most embarrassing afternoon of my life would lay a foundation for body acceptance and understanding that would last a lifetime. At the time, though, it was just an emotional scar that would haunt me until marriage. One of my favorite sayings is "That what doesn't kill you, makes you stronger." On that one afternoon, I became the strongest fourteen-year-old on earth.

Some weeks before, my best friend David and his brother were sent to their cousin's house for the summer. They were off to the good life, playing in the pool, running through the woods, and lounging in the sunset. This, of course, was after they spent a dozen hours a day worming tobacco, weeding tobacco, picking tobacco, and twisting tobacco. For such a young group of boys, they sure spent a lot of time with tobacco products.

Their misfortune was great fortune for me. When David left, he asked me to tend to his paper route. Along with allowing me to keep the profits from the paper route, I would be allowed to use his brand new, paper delivery model bike. Not just for business use, either. I could use it for personal use, as well.

Just picture me pedaling down to the local store to buy candy on the hottest wheels in town, a red Schwinn three speed bike with front and side baskets? I was the king. I thought that paper delivery was the easiest job known to kids. I drop off the paper every afternoon after school and collect the money on Saturday. David did have one other request, though. He wanted me to see if there was some law against converting fourteen years old boys into migrant slave laborers. I promised that I would look into it if I had the time.

The day before David left, he took me around to get used to

the route. He pointed to each house that I was supposed to deliver the paper to, and I marked each mailbox with a piece of tape. We went over the collection procedures. Each house had its own little quirk. Some one thing, then some another. One house had to be collected before ten o'clock because the guy was a little league baseball coach and had games almost all day on Saturday. My favorite stop was Mrs. Smith. She would deny getting all of her papers and refuse to pay.

"You have to get to Mrs. Smith before garbage pickup at noon. If ya don't, she'll say that she didn't get 'em," David warned me. "Also, you have to open Tuesday's paper 'cause she will hide Thursday's in Tuesday's hoping that, since they both start with "T," you won't notice."

When we got to the old house at the end of the road, I put a strip of tape on the mailbox and asked for the collecting instructions. David hesitated, then replied that he didn't collect from them.

I thought this was strange. He delivered the papers, but wasn't collecting the money. I wanted to be polite. I didn't want to pry into his business, but there was just too much curiosity contained in me to let me walk away from this particular situation. I thought perhaps I could bring the subject up again at a better time, however. I waited for almost four seconds.

"How come?" I asked with a puzzled look.

David walked back over to his bike and gestured for us to leave.

"You can collect it if you want. There is four weeks of back money owed," David said. "I'm not going up there."

I delivered the papers faithfully for the first two weeks. I was not able to collect the first Saturday because it poured rain all day. Everyone knows that paper boys can deliver in the rain but are not required to collect in the rain. The second Saturday was warm and sunny, the perfect weather to collect my earnings. I had decided that I would treat myself to an ice cream and a coke at the local drive-in when I finished collecting. I certainly deserved that little pleasure. I also knew that Lora, the beautiful new redhead from science class, would be there. I was certain that there would be money left over after paying the paper bill to worm my way into her heart by plying her with carbonated beverages and frozen dairy products.

No one pays the paper boy. Paper boys have to develop skills necessary for collecting money from the worst dead-beats in the neighborhood. You have to be part actor, liar, and enforcer to meet the challenges put before the collector. Collecting for the newspaper has been considered as a college education for the banking and loan sharking industry. If you have been a paper boy for more than two years, then the mob wants you to be the trainer in their collections department.

I set out, armed with the information that David had given me, along with the knowledge gathered by living in this neighborhood for several years. Being new at the job, I stumbled through my first round of collecting.

The first stop was relatively easy. The family had only been getting the paper for a few months and hadn't gotten enough experience to master their technique, yet. I walked up to the door and banged sufficiently loud enough so as to insure that, if they all had died during the night, they still would hear me at the door. I banged again and hollered for Mr. Bill to come to the door and pay me. It wasn't until the third time I banged on the door that I realized they were avoiding me. Thinking quickly, I shouted to them that I had to leave, but I would leave the Saturday Special Edition on the front porch and would return later.

I pretended to stomp my way down the steps, then hid behind

their wicker chair. Mr. Bill stuck his nose out of the door slowly, peering left and right to make sure that I was gone. When he reached out to get the fake paper, I slapped his hand with my bill. "A dollar-fifty please," I said. He shrugged and handed me the money. I knew he would not fall for this trick the next time, however.

Some people fell for the same tricks week after week. I'd go to Old Mrs. Sophie's and yell, "Drug Store!" She would come out with money in her hand. Mr. Taylor would come to the door in a flash if you shouted, "Liquor Store!" The hardest to collect was Mr. Jones, that is, until I started asking him why I always saw his car parked at Miss Lisa's house on the nights that told his wife that he was working late. After that I got a tip every week. He would hunt me down to pay me. Sometimes twice, just to make sure that I didn't come around the house, again.

House after house, I knocked. I tried every trick that David had given me. I collected about half of the houses, a little better than David had said I would do, but a little less than I had planned on. I needed twelve dollars to pay for next week's papers and I needed at least three dollars for the ice cream plans. I just didn't have enough for both the girl and me. I was certain that I was not going to be the one left out, but I really wanted to see Lora.

It had come down to the last house. If I got the money from the last house, I would not only have enough money for the ice cream scheme, but I would have enough for a follow-up date. We all know that it's the follow-up date that asserts your claim on going together. What it never asserted to me was where you are going or what you are going to do when you get there. If I collected from that house, though, I was certain that I would find out.

It was a spooky old place. The clapboard siding was in need of paint, and the tin roof was a dull shade of rust. The yard was closed off from view. The trees were bare of leaves. The place was in need of paint. Scariest of all was the fact that no one really knew the people that moved into the place after Old Man Tom died.

It was the money that made me strong enough to go up there to collect the back bills. The money would supply the means for getting close to Lora. After all, what good is a job if it doesn't provide the means to getting closer to the prettiest girl in town?

I pedaled the bike up the long driveway and walked it up to the gate that sat at the front of the lawn. I pushed the button on the intercom and announced that I was the paper boy and I was there to collect the weekly fee. A short buzzing sound permitted the gate to swing free from its catch. I pushed the gate open and wheeled my bike inside. I kept my bike with me, even up on the porch, just in case I needed to make a fast getaway. As the lady of the house opened the front door, I trembled with fear.

She stood at the front door wearing a terry cloth bath robe. I thought about how much she looked like my mother and not the menacing ghoul that I had imagined. Her hair was wet, and she looked like she hadn't yet dressed for the day, but mostly she looked like everyone else in the world. I apologized for the bill being so high and explained that no one had collected all month. She chuckled and handed me a twenty-dollar bill.

That was the first twenty-dollar bill that I had ever owned. Now, of course, I had to find a way to make change for the fare. I explained to the lady that I would have to go to the store and get her change. She just waved and replied that she would be in the rear by the swimming pool.

"Just ring the bell, and I'll come back around the front and meet you," she said with a smile.

All the way to Frank's Store I thought about how nice this lady was to trust me to return with her change. I thought how nice it was that this lady had a pool. I thought how nice it would be if she let me swim there, especially if she would let me bring Lora. I thought of—well, from that point on, my thoughts mostly surrounded Lora's red bikini. I am really not sure if she had one, but I am sure that she would have looked great in it.

Frank's Store was buzzing with people stopping off to get milk and bread, mingle between the shoppers, and gather the latest gossip. I wandered up to the register to ask Mr. Frank for change for the twenty-dollar bill. He peered over his wire rimmed glasses with a gaze that could pierce steel.

"Where did you get a twenty-dollar bill?" he asked in his gruff voice.

"From the lady at the end of Smithfield Drive," I said. "She is paying her paper bill."

Mr. Frank rolled his eyes. The rest of the store stopped mingling. For the first time in years, the gossiping stopped. They leaned their ears closer and strained their eyes to catch a glimpse of this conversation.

Frank handed me three fives and five ones. I walked out of the store, dodging the litter of people staring at me. As I exited the building, I could hear the gossip machine beginning to whine away in the background.

I boarded my bike and pedaled my way back to the house. I was curious why the whole store had stopped talking when I mentioned the house. I thought perhaps that it was because they were all jealous of the lady's swimming pool. I never decided if that was correct, as my mind wandered down to the house, to the pool, and to the red bikini, again.

I reached the gate again and rang the bell. I rang it a second time after waiting quite a while. When I reached up to ring the bell again, I noticed that the gate had not latched when I left the first time. I pushed the gate open and rolled the bike up to the porch.

The smart thing to do would have been to go to the front door and ring the door bell. I have been accused of a lot of things in my life, but doing the smart thing is not one of them. I thought that it would be more expedient to just go around back to find the nice lady. As much as anything else, I wanted to see the pool.

I saw that the circular drive was full of cars. I also noticed it was laundry day from all of the clothes hung on hangers all across the front porch rails. Walking around the front corner of the house, I could hear the laughter of the crowd and the splashing of the what sounded like pool water. The closer I got, the more the fun crept toward me.

As I turned the corner, there sat the most beautiful pool that I had ever seen. Big and blue and full of cool water. I stood there gazing at this wonderful pool as a naked body drifted past my line of sight.

Naked? I looked again. Still naked.

The lady was ancient. She was thirty-five years old if she was a day. It was like looking at my mother. I thought how odd for a mother-type lady with a flabby butt and a sagging chest to be at the pool all nude and stuff. Certainly the pool was the domain of skinny eighteen-year-old blonde lifeguard types, and even they were not naked.

I came to realize that everyone was naked. The lady that I was supposed to collect from, her husband, and all of the guests were walking around without a stitch of clothing. I thought to myself that perhaps I should lay the change on the snack table and run. Just about the time that I was about to implement this plan, the lady of the house approached me. I was caught.

"It's not nice to enter a person's home without knocking young man," she said sternly.

With a grimace, she held out her hand to take the money. I wish that I had known that she was reaching for the money. If I had, I probably would not have screamed. I probably would not have had to hold so tightly to my water, either. Thinking quickly, I decided that a running plan was called for immediately. I shifted my brain into panic mode, and my feet into quick mobile mode.

A strange thing happened on the way to the bike. I crashed directly into Lora. The most beautiful girl that I had ever considered asking for ice cream was laying flat on the ground and blocking my exit. I think that I might have suffered some brain damage in the crash, also. It wasn't until after I had helped her up and brushed the dirt from the seat of her pants that I realized that she was wasn't wearing pants. She wasn't wearing anything for that matter.

Ever have a wave of Hot Molten Stupid rise in your body? You know, the kind that starts at your feet and makes its way up to your brain, then spills out of your mouth? I think that this was the very first time that this happened to me. Unfortunately, it was not the last. I buried my thoughts in not saying anything stupid, but stupid was all that would come out.

"Sorry for naking you off," I said. "I mean, naking you up. No, knocking you up."

Now, I knew that this wasn't right. I also knew that if I struggled long enough, I could find the right words.

"No, helping," I said. "I'm sorry for helping you up."

I could see in her face that she was enjoying my clumsy attempt at an apology. That maniacal young girl was actually getting pleasure from my awkwardness. This was to be my first lesson in Women 101, the lesson that teaches you that all women get some sadistic pleasure out of watching men in the process of looking stupid. This could be the only reason that women marry men, just for this pleasure.

I kept stumbling through the apology until I think that I might have apologized for assassinating Kennedy. In the midst of complete self-destruction, I caught a glimpse of the twinkle in her eyes. Before my very eyes, I watched as she melted into a normal, ordinary girl with wonderful eyes. I could see that she was still naked, but the same young girl that I saw at school every day. She was not the naked girl at the scary lady's house, but just an ordinary, everyday beauty queen from the neighborhood.

It was about this time that I realized that most of my past thoughts of Lora had involved this unsuspecting girl in various stages of skimpy dress, a cheerleader outfit or a swimsuit. I realized that, although she was completely naked now, she was less attractive sexually than when I had imagined her scantily clothed. Today, I saw her as a human being.

I thought about how glad I was not to have to worry about an uncontrollable erection at this moment. I was amazed to find that I was standing next to the lady of my dreams, and that she was totally naked. I thought about how embarrassing it would be to develop an erection just like when I visualized her in that red bikini. That gorgeous, red, skimpy bikini.

Most everyone has heard the expression, "Mention the devil, and there he is." Such was the case here. As the thoughts of embarrassment were creeping into my brain, a horizontal tent was being erected in my pants.

As the tent pole reached full extension, that once friendly but now scary lady, Mrs. Delcie, grabbed me by the shoulder. Not harsh or rough, but firm enough that thoughts of running didn't seem practical.

"I see you met my daughter," the lady said.

I said yes and turned to face the lady. It is tough enough to meet a girl's parents without having to meet the girl's completely naked parents. Most guys get to start out with just meeting the dressed version. If things go well, he doesn't ever have to meet the naked version, at least not until after being married to the girl for many decades. Then, he only meets the naked version at the old age home where the parents are probably senile and don't even realize that they are naked.

I wasn't quite sure how Lora's mom was going to react to the situation, with her and her daughter being naked and all. I certainly didn't want to be caught staring at Lora. I didn't know where to look. I decided that the best thing to do was to look directly at her mom's face. This probably would have worked better if I hadn't just realized that Mrs. Delcie was just an older version of Lora with larger breasts, and, of course, still naked. At this point, I figured that I was in for it anyway, so I might as well look where I happened to look.

I wheeled around, tent pole and all, and locked onto Mrs. Delcie's eyes. To my surprise, she didn't kill me. She didn't even look upset. She talked quietly with me, explaining that they were nudists and believed that the human body was nothing to be ashamed of. I think that there was some other stuff, too, but I was trying to concentrate on making the Indians remove their teepee.

Since the Indians didn't seem to want to cooperate, my next plan was to close my eyes and think, *I am invisible! I AM invisible! I am INVISIBLE!*

That didn't seem to work, either. Mrs. Delcie kept on talking, and no one seemed to be reacting to a young boy vanishing before their eyes. I moved to the next plan. This one consisted of praying that a large earthquake would hit and swallow me up.

God didn't answer that particular prayer, but He did give me what I needed and lowered the flag pole to half mast. I quickly thanked God and continued searching for a way out of this mess.

Mrs. Delcie had to attend to her guests, but promised me that I was in good hands with Lora. She invited me to sit down and stay for a while. I must have had some of that Hot Molten Stupid still floating around in my body. It again rushed my brain and spilled out into my mouth. Without the slightest bit of cognizant thought, I blurted out that I didn't have a swim suite, and that I was sure that I had left it at my house. I started racing toward the bike. As I jumped aboard, I could hear Lora saying goodbye.

The bike ride home was fast and stress relieving. The harder I pedaled, the better I felt. I was beginning to understand that I would never get to have the ice cream with Lora, but I think that it was for the best. How in the world could I explain having a girlfriend that never wore clothes? Mom certainly would never let her in the house without some type of covering. Dad would simply beat me until there was nothing left to dress.

It never occurred to me that nudists were only naked when appropriate. They were dressed for things like visiting a neighbor or going out for ice cream. As a young teen, I had a lot to learn about nudism. I was still thinking that if Lora and I ever got to go together, we would have to go everywhere with her as bare as the day she was born. I had no idea how to explain this to my parents.

I didn't know how this was going to work out. Going to the store with Lora wearing nothing but a suntan would be somewhat embarrassing. Sauntering into church and sitting down on the middle row pew would certainly raise a few eyebrows. I was glad that my Mom didn't know a thing about this situation. She would not understand, being old and prudish.

When I reached the house, my mother was sitting on the front porch, rocking in her favorite chair. I put the bike away on the car port, walked over to Mom, and sat down on the chair beside her. We both rocked for a few minutes without talking.

With a calm voice, Mom asked how the collecting went, and if there were any problems along the way. I replied that everything went smoothly. I, of course, didn't want to worry her with the details of the day, so I didn't mention the recent unpleasantness. I was certain that Mom didn't need to know the details of my incident with the new family. It might cause a scene, something that no teen wants.

Out of the blue, Mom said that she understood that I had met the new people down the block. A small pause in her speech indicated that Mom knew something, but I couldn't be sure. She continued on that she thought that my dad and she might walk down there after lunch and introduce themselves. At this point, I knew that she was fishing for a response from me.

I had two choices. The first choice was to admit that I had spent the afternoon in the company of several nude adults and at least one very attractive teenage female and suggest that they avoid the location. The other choice was to let them go down there and see for themselves just what was happening. They would also want to know why I had not said anything. I was trapped in what is now known throughout the county as "Bud's Quandary." Either I tell them not to go there and have to try to explain what I was doing hanging out with a bunch of naked people, or I send them down to the naked people, and they will walk head first into a sea of "nudie" people. After struggling for several nervous seconds, a third idea popped into my head.

I could just not answer. Neither of the first two choices seemed like a great idea. I went with the third option.

As days go, I was having extremely poor luck with my choices. Every escape plan seemed to blow up in my face. This plan was no exception. Although I had planned to not say anything and just walk into the house, my mouth had not received those particular instructions and blurted out something to the effect that the walk would do them good. At this point I was certain that I had overdosed on that Hot Molten Stupid in the middle of the night and that I would probably die of it before the day ended.

As I pulled the screen door open, my mother stopped me with those piercing mother eyes of hers, causing my legs to freeze in the still position. She never moved her eyes from the magazine that she was reading, never changed the tone of her voice or diverted her attention from the mid morning break. She just used that mental "Mom Brake" that freezes kids in their tracks for no apparent reason.

"You wouldn't let your mother go to a place filled with naked people, would you?" she finally asked.

I was caught, again. I was ratted out by Lora's mom. Mom informed me that Mrs. Delcie had called and explained everything to her. I made a mental note to include in tonight's prayers a request for phone disruption on demand. That prayer request was, of course, denied. Substituted in its place was a prohibition on use of the phone for two weeks. Attached to that particular prohibition was one on sitting. That prohibition was mostly physical and was short lived. The pain subsided not long after Dad returned the belt to the loops in his pants.

The week-long grounding went quickly. I was still allowed to deliver the papers and to run errands. I just couldn't have any fun. I learned to make the best of it, though. I considered the paper route to be a freeing experience. It was fun to ride the bike, and I could pretend that I was flying a bomber, delivering bombs to the enemy mailboxes. Making work a game made the grounding somewhat more enjoyable. Saturday arrived soon enough.

I returned to collecting for the paper in the normal style, using every trick that I could conceive. When I reached Lora's house, I pedaled up to the mailbox and found an envelope with my name on it, just as Mom and Mrs. Delcie had arranged. When I opened it, there was a check for the paper plus twenty-five cents extra. Also, there was a ten-dollar bill and with a note attached to it. Mrs. Delcie had felt partly responsible for the trouble that I was in and wanted me to have the ten-dollar bill for my troubles.

I tucked the money in my pocket. The check was worthless, as far as I was concerned. I would have to get one of my parents to cash it. That insured that the money would go to pay the bill at the newspaper office and that the residual would migrate into the nebulous college fund. When you are fourteen, a college fund is next to useless. You can't spend it. You can't even take it out and play with it. It really doesn't exist.

The ten-dollar bill was like found money. No one but me knew about it. It was ready cash, designed for spending immediately. No one could stop me from blowing it on candy, baseball cards, or other important things like that. I thought at first about going to the movies. I had enough money that I could take David with me and still have enough for candy and drinks. The only glitch in this plan was that David was hundreds of miles away, and, of course, the part of my plan where I click my heels together and chant, "There's no place like the movies," didn't bring him back.

I briefly considered the possibility of calling on Lora for

that first attempt at a date. I am not sure if I was insane at the time, or if I had come to enjoy the pain and embarrassment that I had inflicted upon myself at our first encounter. Coming to my senses, I decided to pedal to the ice cream shop and have a sundae, or two, or four.

Sitting alone at the corner booth of the ice cream store was Lora. There was a loneliness in her face. The sadness could be seen as she stared out the window. I walked over to her table and motioned a hello with my hand. Her eyes glimmered when she smiled at me.

I thought that I would finally get my ice cream date with her until that stupid fluid filled my head again. I valiantly resisted the fluid as it tried to escape out of my mouth, but at the last minute, the dam broke. Utter gibberish flowed from my mouth and descended upon her with the force of a tidal wave. She smiled and asked me to join her. At this moment, I realized that she spoke gibberish. Even today, I admire that trait in a woman.

Now I had my chance to show her my smooth style and graceful approach. As it turned out though, I didn't have either. That was all right, though. She just wanted to tell me a little about her family and friends. She wanted to explain to me about nudism. Most of all, she wanted to ask me not to go blabbing my mouth to all of my friends that I had seen her naked. She was still a teenager and didn't want to be the brunt of all of the teenage boys' jokes. I think that it was mostly the begging me not to tell that gave me the opportunity to sit with Lora and talk.

Looking at her puppy dog eyes, I couldn't refuse her request. It meant that I could not brag to all of the guys that I was the first of the group to see a live non-relative female form completely naked. I had felt a little uneasy talking about it. I probably wouldn't have said anything anyway.

I ordered ice cream for the two of us. We stayed at the ice cream shop for hours talking and laughing. She told me about the different people that she had met during the family's nudist vacations. She amused me with tales swimming naked in the pool, the unique feeling of the cool water flowing over her body, and how the warm sun felt on her skin. Lora even invited me to come over to the next party and skinny dip with them.

The time went fast, but as sure as there is an Indian tribe in my pants, there had to be an end to our conversation. I had spent many nights thinking about this event. Now that it was coming to a close, I had to think of a way to move this relationship into a dating format. As most of my plans had blown up in my face, I decided just to wing it. Whatever happened, would happen.

I knew that when we left, she would have to walk home. I worked the "Can I walk you home?" question into the conversation. If there was only one smooth line that I had to deliver, this was it. Smooth and flawless, the words rolled off of my tongue. They drifted across the noisy room and landed squarely on her naked ear. She smiled and accepted.

As we walked, I tried my best to work up the nerve to reach out and hold her hand. The first attempt ended in folly. I tripped during the execution, and I ended up holding her pocketbook zipper fob. Both useful objects, but not exactly the same. The second attempt forced me to take two lateral steps to get close enough to her arm to reach her hand. I became amazed at how quickly the ground approaches when you step on your own sneaker. Looking as cool as possible, I began to stand up. She reached out her hand and helped me to my feet.

Staring at me with those sadistic eyes, she said, "Sorry for knocking you up."

Success at last. Now I had a firm grip on her soft velvet

skinned fingers. Perhaps I held on a little too tightly at first. The slight purplish tint to her hand was my first clue. Still, I was afraid to loosen my grip for fear that she would use that opportunity to snatch her hand away from mine. I had worked so hard to get to this point that nothing as small as a purple hand would deter me.

We climbed the steps onto the porch at her front door. She reached out and kissed me on the cheek. Prying her hand from my grip, she smiled at me and told me what a good friend I was going to make. The rest of the conversation wandered on about her being able to talk to me about nudism and other stuff. I am not sure exactly what she said, but I am sure it wasn't "Do you want to go steady?"

I knew that the "friends" thing was the death nail in any "going together," but I never found out where we were going, anyway. We did talk often about the traps of teenage life and the pitfalls of this boyfriend and that girlfriend. It worked out for the best. I needed a good friend.

Nudist Soup

Ever notice what the most used piece of equipment is at a nudist resort? When you walk through the park, you will see an unused weight machine, a slightly used stationary bicycle, and a set of free weights rusting in the corner. The hot tub, of course, is full to the brim with patrons swirling around the water and several people standing on the fringes conversing with each other while waiting their turn to get in. It certainly is one of the more popular spots at the resorts.

I am fond of the hot tubs, too, although they conjure strange images of cannibalistic cartoons in my mind. Ever see the Bugs Bunny cartoon where the witch has Bugs in the cauldron and is busy adding carrots and potatoes to the mix? Or can you imagine a group of natives in jungle preparing a missionary for dinner?

While lounging in my own hot tub and hiding from my wife's "honey do" list, I discovered just how real that vision was, metaphorically speaking. We take bubbling water, mix in a few choice "meatings," add a spicy conversation or two, and soon we have a nudist soup.

The nudists are the meat of these soups. We supply the bulk and consistency to the soup. We give the soup its strongest flavor. Perhaps that is why we call a group of people sitting around not accomplishing anything a meeting.

You can tell the beef people from the others from their bullish attitude. They storm in the tub and begin to sling ideas around. Its not until one of their ideas hits the fan that the soup bowl empties out. Of course the chickens just sit there and peck at what was said. Then there are the ones whose stories seem to be based on the truth, but you are not really sure if it's possible. You know that they are concocting a fishy soup.

I don't like the vegetable soups either. They are the ones that just sit there like sacks of potatoes, or stop all conversation with their onion sneer. I find that, no matter how hot the water is, their soup seems rather cold. There is one exception, though. Just toss in a fruit or some nuts and a few flakes, and now you've got a worthy stew. Add too many of them, though, and you end up with a nudist granola bar. They are the nudist equivalent of tofu burgers on bran muffins.

I think that my favorite nudist soup is the nudist duck soup, a pot full of people splashing around with a quack or two thrown in for good luck. Crumble in a few crackers and some saucy conversation, and dinner is served.

Sometimes, the conversation is just too spicy for me. I like the hot Texas Pete conversations like religion, politics, and body piercing, but I usually get a sick feeling in my stomach later from all that turmoil. The zesty salsa talks intrigue me, also, especially the ones that begin, "Ever wonder what the world would be like if there wasn't ...?" Its good to revel in those what if's, but it certainly can give you a headache.

You can always tell which meat is absorbing the most sauce, too. They are the ones that sit comfortably at the back of the pot and smile as the rest of us stir about the pot grumbling. The least tasty pieces are the ones that only allow their thoughts to be heard. I guess that I fall in the middle, with just enough spices to make me interesting, but not enough to increase the sales of Tums.

Like any good soup, you can always tell when the soup is especially good. When the soup leaves a good taste in your mouth and you leave wishing you could have just a little more, you know it was a good nudist soup.

An Isaiah Afternoon

To: Mr. Christian, Financial Officer of Wool Ridge Full Gospel, Bible Believing, Full Immersion Baptist Church of Lower Saint Matthews Ridge.
Re: Request for Budget Items for the Coming Year.

Dear Mr. Christian,

In response to your request for more information concerning my request for $2000.00, I have written this response. I realize that on the form that I sent you I listed the reason only as "Prayer, Bible Study, Bail, and Attorney Money," but it seemed better to give a short answer at the time. I now see the necessity of expanding my explanation to include a few more details. I would ask that you please keep our correspondence about this incident between the two of us. I am sure you will understand once you read this response.

It all started last Wednesday. It was a beautiful crisp morning. The sun shone in the bedroom window, and the clouds drifted through as little pillows. My wife was still asleep, so I eased out of bed and shuffled into the kitchen. I fixed a cup of coffee and sat at the kitchen table, thumbing through the Bible and searching for a phrase to jump out at me.

I often just leaf through the Bible and let the Spirit tell me where to begin. I have found this to be a wonderful way to maintain a lighthearted devotional in the morning. It is especially helpful on those days when my wife is still asleep and I am alone in my solace. The peace and quiet are only broken by the beep of the coffee pot and the clinking of the spoon in the mug. But I digress.

That Wednesday began wonderfully. First a passage in Psalms, then one in Proverbs, but that was way too heavy a rebuke for such a lazy Wednesday. Next, I came across Isaiah and the instructions from God to remove his sack cloth and sandals and walk about the nation preaching of God's rebuke. Now I had something to sink my teeth into. Sipping my coffee, I savored every word. I thought how intense Isaiah's trust in God must have been.

I could only imagine the look on people's faces today if a prophet walked down Main Street, naked, preaching the good news of Christ. As I basked in my new excitement, and while mindlessly thumbing the pages again, I found the passage, "Go and do likewise."

I thought for a moment just how funny it would be if God was telling me to go out in the world proclaiming the gospel naked. As a leafed through a few more pages, I saw before me the passage in the first chapter of James, "Be ye doers of the Word."

I pondered the significance of that statement. The word said to go and do as Isaiah had done. It said for me to walk through my Jerusalem without the benefit of clothes. Wow, what a rush.

I slammed the Bible shut. I slammed my eyes shut. And before me, in the darkness, I could see myself waving a Bible over my head and preaching the gospel in my birthday suit. I almost fainted. Surely there was some mistake.

I opened the Bible again. I was certain that I had just gotten the wrong verses and that God would send me the correct one now and all of this would go away and that at the end of the next verse that I would see the final blessing that I was searching for.

As the pages fell open, there it was. "What thou doest, doest thou quickly."

Well, there I was, standing in the kitchen, holding my cup of coffee, and in my brand-new BVD's realizing that I was more dressed now than I would be all day. I thought for a minute, *prayer*. That's it. I should pray for divine insight for these verses. Surely God had a special meaning in those verses, and I had failed to see His plan.

I realized that I had failed to start my day with prayer. So I prayed. Then I prayed. I really prayed. In the midst of all that I prayed and thought, an answer came. "What? Are you too stupid to read for yourself? Or are you too afraid to do what I asked? I made Abraham offer to sacrifice his son. I made Job lose everything. I ask you to walk around in the suit that I gave you, and you freak out."

I am not certain why I was surprised that the voice was Jewish. It was clear; it was pointed; but it was definitely Jewish. I looked in the mirror at the fat, balding, middle-aged guy with the ugly smile. Certainly God didn't mean me.

I said to myself, "How bad could it be?" I planned to stay home all day. No one was supposed to visit. And my son was with his grandad for the day. I stripped down to my birthday suit and announced to the dog and my wife that I would obey God and stay naked all day. The dog was fine with it, but the wife was a little shaken.

All was going fine until the phone rang. My neighbor's son had gotten his toe stuck in the tub drain and needed my help. My wife had just left for the store, and my neighbor's husband was away on a fishing trip. I was all that she had left to help her.

Now, I am all for full disclosure on most things, but this would be full disclosure of "dis- clothing." I was not sure how to begin a conversation about being naked for God with my neighbor and not look like some kook that would soon be on the Jerry Springer Show. I quickly pondered a lengthy discussion on biblical principals and the segue into the naked part. This situation didn't seem to lend itself to short explanations, and I could hear little Johnny screaming in the background. I was certain that I didn't have enough time to explain everything to Mrs. Jones. Besides, it was just next door.

I asked Mrs. Jones to hold on the phone, noting that it may take several minutes to return. I fashioned a plan that involved sneaking in the Jones' back door, creeping into the bathroom, and freeing Johnny's toe without Mrs. Jones knowing a thing. Then, from the safety of my kitchen, I could return to the phone call and say that Johnny was released from the tub's maniacal grip. This would keep Mrs. Jones in the kitchen long enough for me to accomplish the task of unfastening the tub's grip from the boy's toe.

My plan was unfolding well. I exited my house, towel wrapped firmly about the waist. Cautiously, I peered around the corner. The alley was clear. I dashed across the rear yard and leaped over the fence. Ever notice that towels never seem to leap to the same height that their owners do?

I stood in the backyard and stared at my towel that was suspended some five feet in the air and on the wrong side of the fence. I also looked in horror as I saw my precious dog, Flash, charging the flapping towel. It had become a race to see who could reach the towel first, and no matter how much crying of foul I did, I couldn't get Flash to play fair and run only on two feet.

My countenance sank severely as I watched my dog devouring my towel. In a short period of time, all that was left was the Holiday Inn logo and the washing instructions. I did briefly speculate as to the breeding and parentage of the dog, but upon further contemplation of the speculation, it didn't seem like much of an insult for a dog. What would you expect him to be the son of, anyway?

Now, amidst all of this, I hear that same Jewish guy speaking about trust and faith.

Remembering my original plan, I headed for the Jones' back door. To my amazement, the door was wide open. I was sure that God had sent me here and had prepared the way. With catlike motions, I stalked into the bathroom and threw open the door, knocking Mrs. Jones to the floor and unconscious. This one small incident sent Johnny into a crying fit. Who would have thought?

I grabbed Johnny's toe and yanked. I figured, since he was already crying, who would notice a little extra. To my surprise, the toe came loose much easier than expected. So much so that the heel of this angel's foot crashed into my body. You know, the part located between the belly button and the knees, and approximately midship. You know, "Two bells but all is not well."

You can imagine the thoughts that were running through Mrs. Jones' mind when she awoke from her nap to find her son running down the hall crying and a naked man bend over clutching his groin. I know what I imagined that she was imagining at that time, so I bid her a good day and made a hasty retreat.

As I left the house and jumped over that fence again, I realized that a leap of only a couple of inches more would not have been as rough on my already sore testicular area. It is, however, harder to jump while still holding on to one's prized possessions. Lying on my back with some discomfort, I realized that I had accomplished what I had set out to do, AND still had kept my promise to God.

Looking around the backyard, I noticed that the dog was gone. Then it hit me, Kari had mentioned that she would come home to drop off the groceries before heading to my dad's for an evening at the in-law's house along with our son. I had begged off because of my new dress code. I snickered to myself as I thought how easy the rest of the day would be now that I was the only one here. No one even knew that I was home. No one could call me. No one even thought that I was around.

I sauntered over to the back door with a smirk on my face. I was master of my fate and king of my dominion. I boldly grasped the door knob and gave the kingly twist. Funny thing about locked door knobs. They don't respect kings and the like. When I left the house, it seemed silly to take a key with me. Besides, where would I have put it?

In the back of my head, I could hear the same old thing – trust me…try me…

I walked around to all of the windows in the rear of the building. Of course all of them were locked. As I neared the end of the building, I stubbed my toe on a brick that my son had left in the grass. I thought to myself that I was glad for the new pain. I was getting so tired of the other one. I did, however, speculate on the parentage of the brick. It seemed more appropriate this time.

For such occasions as this, we have hidden a key in the flower pot out front. At the time it seemed like the most likely place. It was easy to get to, in plain sight of the street, and hidden in a place that no one would think to look. Glancing at the nothingness that I was wearing, I noticed that it was only a few hours until it would be dark and safe for me to sneak around front and get the key in the safety of darkness.

I decided not to waste the rest of the afternoon fretting over the problems of the morning, but, instead, to take a little nap in the lounge chair while the afternoon sun set. I lay in our chair for a short while. The sun warmed me. I could feel the tensions of the day evaporate. I felt at peace with the world. I could see the clouds drifting by as I drifted into a snooze. I am certain that I could have slept for a few more hours except for the intense pain that I felt as I inadvertently dragged my hand across my now sunburned belly.

Blood curdling screams bellowed from my mouth as I dragged my arm across my bare chest. I didn't realize that you could get so burned in four hours out in the sun. Nor did I realize that the screams had been heard by the police who were scouring the neighborhood looking for a naked pervert with a penchant for young boys' toes.

I decided that it was necessary to try to retrieve the key, even if I risked being spotted by any of the neighbors. I planned to skirt behind the bushes and stretch up to the flower pot that sat in the window box under the bay window. It was a good plan if I do say so myself.

I had great success in the bushes. Even the menacing sticker bushes that my wife had planted to deter burglars were not too rough on my sunburned skin. The guttural groaning could probably be heard by our next door neighbors.

Stretching up toward the window box, I reached as hard as I could to grasp the flower pot. The harder I stretched, the farther the pot seemed. It became obvious that I would have to stand up, take a chance, and risk it all. I closed my eyes and stood long enough to get the pot and drop straight to the ground again.

At first, I thought that the shrill scream of Mrs. Jones was a flash back to this morning until I looked up to see her standing at my door step, ringing the doorbell. She had come over to warn us about the pervert in the neighborhood and to tell us to watch our son like a hawk. It is ironic that she would arrive at that specific moment. Still, I wanted to accomplish my task, so I waved and bid Mrs. Jones a good day, knowing that the ship had probably already sailed.

I knew that if I could just get into the house that the problems would soon be solved. I fumbled through the dirt to find the key. I sifted the dirt through my fingers. I poured the dirt onto the ground, kicking the dirt around looking for the key. Of course, there was no key.

With a throbbing toe, a sore nether region, and a sunburned belly, I decided that I had been through enough. I stood up, walked around the side of the building and grabbed the brick firmly in my hand. Well, the second time. The first time I grabbed the slimy wet brick, I kind of dropped it on my good toes. Now I have a matched set.

With a vengeance only known to an insane sunburned nudist, I flung the brick at the kitchen window, shattering the first pane of glass. I blame the failure of this plan on my wife who insisted on triple pane windows but only bore me a single brick son. To her credit, though, the alarm system seemed to work well. It could not have been more than a few seconds before the kind police officer slammed me to the ground and arrested me.

I did finally find some peace and quiet in the ride to the station in the police car. The trip was uneventful and pleasurable.

It appears as though the cost for defending me at this time is about $2000.00. And as I was on a mission for God, it seems as the church should reimburse me for my out-of-pocket expenses. I have not asked for the cost of replacing the window, the cost of new clothes, or the cost of a hotel stay to glean some new towels. I did wish to lump into this the cost of my divorce attorney, but my wife got custody of the other requisition form.

As it is coming close to budget time again, you might think

of making a small allocation for these types of things in the future. If I can be of any more help in this matter, do not hesitate to call me.

Your servant, Chester.

Response scribbled across the bottom of the page: Chester, ever think that Satan might be Jewish? Denied.

From Girlfriend to Wife

In high school, all boys want the same thing. They want cool cars, cool clothes, and to date the Prom Queen. As we get older, our tastes mature. We want fast cars that are cool, expensive clothes that are cool, and a wife that used to be the Prom Queen and now is the reigning Miss Virginia.

In my high school days, I was no different. I figured that God had a plan for me that would include an award winning wife of unmatched beauty. She would be tall, thin, tanned, and have a great personality, while still being able to maintain her balance with her large chest. She would be the envy of the neighborhood.

I prayed to God, in my most humble way, that my future wife didn't have to be Miss America. The runner up would be sufficient, so long as she was from the South. I think that I even mentioned the little Rebel Flag that should have been tattooed on her lower left backside. In my defense, though, it was the first time that I had prayed for something with the full expectation of an answered prayer.

Some years later, I found my perfect wife. She was short, ordinary, and easily able to balance her abundant endowment. Of all the creatures on earth, Karalyn was the one woman on earth that could survive, and even thrive, while being married to me. As much as I searched, though, I could not find the Rebel Flag anywhere on her body. I guess that I shouldn't have been surprised that a Yankee would not have such a symbol, though.

What did surprise me was that God had given me what I

needed to do the tasks are awaiting me on earth. He gave me someone that was good with finances, fairly good natured, and pleasant to be around. He gave me a wife that was capable of correcting my shortcoming. Together, we make a complete package.

One of the characteristics that endears me to Karalyn is her ability to follow me into endless numbers of adventures with only the slightest flinch in her expression. Her face never betrays the emotions that must be raging through her mind as she surveys the expanses of my inquisitive thoughts and desires. She would make an excellent poker player.

As a nudist, I wear clothes when necessary. If it is cold out, I wear clothes. If I am going to be in the presence of textile compulsive people, I wear clothes. When appropriate, I wear clothes. When I can, I go without the bondage of clothing.

When we married, however, Karalyn wore clothes all of the time. She wore them to bed. She wore them to swim. She wore them to the dinner table. She wore them to do laundry. I'm not sure, but I think that she wore clothes in the shower, too.

Imagine her expression as I walked in the door of our first apartment for the first time, stripped down to nothing, took a shower, and proceeded to sit at the table for dinner naked. I think that "shocked" was a mild form of the words that described all of the expressions that flowed across Karalyn's face.

Nudism is an integral part of my life. To my wife, however, her husband, the resident nut and overall kooky nudist, is an integral part of her life. This presented Karalyn with a problem that seemed to present two solutions.

Option one was to ignore the naked lump on the couch and see if he would ever grow up, get dressed, get a normal job, and become an adult. After nine years, Karalyn finally gave up and opted for option two.

Option two consisted of trying nudism for herself. This, of course, flew in the face of her Yankee Presbyterian upbringing. With the fortitude of steel, she screwed on her stoic face and headed off to the local nudist park for some summer relaxation and fun. I'm not sure that she liked it as much as she was relieved that not all nudists are compulsive and unrestrained.

Along the nudist way, Karalyn and I have been working through the different little snags that come with any adventure. It was much easier once Karalyn discovered that not all nudists were as bizarre as her husband. She found that many nudists were just plain, ordinary people that liked being nude and also liked being around and interacting with others. The rest just fell into place.

Some sixteen years later, Karalyn is a normal well-adjusted nudist wife. She has been a willing participant in many adventures, encounters, and projects. It is not often that a person finds a woman quite like Karalyn.

I am not sure if I am just lucky or smart, or if God took pity on this lamppost-dumb creature. It has taken me years to find out what God knew all along. Karalyn is the perfect match for me. She may not have a rebel flag on her backside or a balance problem based on the size of her chest, but God did give me the one thing that I needed most from my wife. Karalyn has the ability to understand me.

Massage Therapy

One of the great treasures of my life has been the gift of a wonderful wife. God surely knew what He was doing assigning such a thoughtful and temperate woman to the task of being my help mate. In the strange moments that all marriages have, she seems to be the solitary person that can withstand my genius.

One such moment of genius came when I read of a Marriage Retreat for nudists in the hills of West Virginia. It sounded great. The sun was shining down on the lush green grass as we lounged by the pool and received sage instruction from two pastors. Actually, I was more interested in the lounging by the pool and escape from the phones than I was the retreat, but it seemed like a good excuse for Karalyn and me to run off for a mini vacation.

We packed up the old camper and trundled off to the retreat. The trip up the hill was not as eventful as some we have survived. It was actually stress relieving for me. Of course, it was stress acquiring for Karalyn. She never seems to enjoy the drive to anywhere. As we pulled into the park, I think Karalyn slid into a relaxing mode.

One of the reasons for choosing this particular event was a massage clinic that was being held on the second and last day. Everyone loves a massage, especially my wife. I figured that I would attend one or two classes, become an expert, and head home, confident that I had become a master masseur and giver of great pleasure. My wife would be proud.

The class was wonderful. Dan made it look so easy. You

just follow the simple "S-O-C-K" method, and nothing can go wrong. Stroke first, then do the outing stroke, next the circle strokes, and finish with the kneading strokes. How hard could this stuff be? Dan seemed to be making his wife happy and relaxed. *I can do this*, I thought.

After Karalyn and I got back from the retreat, my mind was filled with great ideas to fulfill my great expectations. I was so excited to finally have a talent to share with my wife that I knew she would enjoy. I decided that the first massage session should be special. I wanted it to be an evening that she would never forget.

As it happened, my son was going to be away for the weekend with my mother, doing all the things that grandmothers do with their grandsons. It was the perfect time to have our special night together. Since I had to take Friday off to take Ajay to his grandmother's anyway, I decided that I would go all out. I would fix a gourmet dinner, complete with soft music and candles. Next, I would clear a space in our bedroom and set up an area for massages. She was going to enjoy this.

Friday arrived quicker than I had anticipated. Funny, during this particular week, Friday came immediately after Thursday. I tried to get a small extension of the week, but God seemed to want the week to stay like He had planned it. I hadn't the time to collect all of the supplies that I needed for the Friday night massage, but I figured that I could improvise as necessary. After all, I was a master masseur now.

Karalyn left for work, and I packed Ajay into the car and sped away. At the first corner, we turned around and returned to the house. Ajay got out of the car and fetched his suitcase from the spot on the porch where he had left it. Returning to the car, I asked him if he needed to go to the restroom. He sighed and replied that he was fine until I had brought it up.

I dropped him off at grandmother's house and sped toward home. I was running approximately on time, but I wanted to have a little time left over to sit in the hot tub and relax before preparing dinner. As I turned into the driveway, I noticed that the trash man had come early, and I had not put the garbage cans out. Hoping to catch him up the street, I slung the cans into the truck and raced down the street after him.

I think that our trash collector delights in seeing us chase him. I blew the horn, flashed my lights, and waved my arms out of the windows, trying to get his attention. It wasn't until he was caught behind a school bus that I was able to pull up behind him and start running toward the back of the truck with my cans. I am certain that I heard the guy on the rear shouting to the driver to hurry up and that I was almost there.

About the time I was about to pour the trash into the back, the bus closed its door, and the trash truck leaped forward, allowing my trash to spill all over the street. I stood on our garbage covered street as the trash truck sped down the road with the guy on the back laughing hysterically. Of course, God thankfully didn't answer my prayer, and the man remained on the bumper until the truck was safely out of sight.

I picked up my trash and returned to the car. I drove back to my house, a little disturbed, but nonetheless driven for a great evening with my wife. I bounded into the house and grabbed the key to the garage. I made my way into the back of the garage where all of the unfinished projects from years past reside. As I passed the mangled piles of debris, I noticed the lethal injections table that I had bought at the state penitentiaries' auction some years ago. It had a head rest, arm supports, and leg supports, everything a person needs for a good massage table. It even had restraints, so there was no possibility of falling off. I carried the plane-shaped table up to the house. After a little cleaning and dusting, I made room for it in our bedroom. I thought a few minutes before I threw out Karalyn's makeup table, but I figured it was a sacrifice that she was willing to make. After all, I gave up my deer antler hat rack. It seemed like an equal deal. Besides, what good is a makeup table since I had to throw out the makeup cabinet to fit the massage table in the room? I did, however, think that Karalyn might be upset with the arm support size holes in the bedroom wall. I would probably be asked to fix those immediately.

With the table set up, I headed to the kitchen to make dinner. I had planned on serving rib eye steak, salad, home fries, and apple pie for dessert. Planned might be a small lie. That was the meal that could be made from the raw material found in the refrigerator and the cupboards. Still, it seemed like a fitting meal for this special occasion.

Exhausted from the morning and midday events, I decided that I needed a break. I turned on the hot tub and returned to the kitchen for my Pepsi and a small cupcake.

When the water was hot, I submerged my body in the blissful water. I laid back and let the water relax me. I could feel the day's tension floating away, swirling around the blue water and into the filter. I have often wondered if the filter ever resented having all this tension sent its way. I guess that is why you have to change them so often.

After what seemed like only a few minutes, the three o'clock train came buzzing by. For most people, the three o'clock train should come at three o'clock, but here in Coalboro, the three o'clock train comes at five fifteen. I was so late. Karalyn would be home in an hour and a half, and I hadn't even started dinner. Springing from the tub, I pulled the door open and headed toward the kitchen. I really wished that my feet had kept up with me at this point, instead of waiting around to see if they could get stuck in the door. You cannot imagine the pain involved in having a foot caught in the door, while plummeting to the floor with the rest of your body, unless you have experienced it personally. I would recommend something else though, if you are given the choice. I thought that it was fortunate that the glass coffee table was situated nearby and in the direct path of my descent. This allowed the breaking glass to slow my descent to the carpet.

I formulated a plan to make the dinner go quickly. All I had to do was start everything all at once, and the meal would be ready in plenty of time. I pulled the deep fat fryer from the cabinet and filled it with oil. I plugged it in and set the oil temperature to high. I figured that it would cook faster that way. I placed the skillet on the stove and cranked the burner to high. I poured the last bit of oil into the pan and dragged the steaks from the freezer. I left the frozen pie in the freezer. I thought that I would have plenty of time to nuke it while we ate. I took the salad stuff from the vegetable crisper, and placed it all on the counter. It was at this point that I noticed that we were low on bacon bits. Not wanting anything to be wrong with this meal, I decided to make my own. I already had the pan hot, and I figured that it would only take a minute to fry the bacon, so I slammed the entire frozen slab into the hot oil.

At this point, I would like to interject a safety tip. Never slam a slab of cold, wet bacon into a skillet of very hot oil when you are naked.

My first reaction was to pour cold water on the effected area. Second safety tip, never spill cold water into a hot skillet with oil in it. As I peeled the layer of oil stained skin from my groin area, I thought how those two safety tips would have made this evening a bit more enjoyable had someone bothered to make these simple rules available to me earlier. Perhaps

OSHA should have a safety booklet for such ideas.

By the time that I had composed myself, the bacon was crispy and brown. I placed the bacon on a paper towel to drain. It was time for the steaks to go into the skillet. My plan was to make everything finish at the same time, so I knew that the home fries had to go in now also. I placed the steaks in the skillet and wheeled my now cautious body around towards the deep fat fryer. It was at this point that I noticed that the plastic lid that covers the oil in the fryer was missing. I was sure that I had placed it back on the fryer after I put the oil in. With nothing else to do but to keep going, I tossed the fries into the fryer.

I wish to reinforce the first safety tip again, but to amend it to include potato products.

I am glad to state though that I was able to locate the lid, as part of the melted plastic from the lid splattered out with the oil and contacted an area that may not be as receptive to melted plastic as it has been to latex and rubber. After speculating about the pot's gender and species, I returned my attention to the steaks. They were beautiful. They were bronze on the top, pink in the middle, and a crispy around the edge. I placed them on our plates and set them on the table.

I chopped lettuce for the salad. I chopped green peppers. I chopped raw spinach. Then I sliced. I sliced onions. I sliced tomatoes. I sliced olives. I bitted. I turned bacon into bacon bits. I turned stale toast into toast bits. And last, I grated. I grated the blue cheese. I grated the Parmesan cheese. I grated my knuckles, only to finish off by grating my last nerve. I tossed this two-gallon concoction into a two-quart mixing bowl. After cleaning up the spilled residue, I placed the salad on the dining room table. I think that it was at this point that I noticed the loaf of Italian bread sitting next to the toaster oven. I had forgotten it. The package said that it took ten minutes in a conventional oven, and Karalyn was going to be home any time now. It occurred to me then that the microwave oven was suppose to be much faster than our regular oven, and I didn't have to wait for it to heat up.

I couldn't find anywhere on the package how long to microwave the bread for, but I did see some toaster oven times that looked as if they would work. I grabbed the bread by the plastic wrapper and forced it into the toaster. I set the timer for four minutes and headed for the den for a small rest. As I passed the fryer, I could see that the home fries had a dark look to them. As I pulled the basket from the oil, it became obvious that the plastic lid had cooked a little too long. The fries looked just like the deep fat fried cheese experiment I tried a few weeks before. At least that was my story, and yes, I stuck to it.

Well, the dinner was ready just as Karalyn pulled into the drive. I thanked God that He allowed me to survive the cooking portion of the evening and confirmed my promise to help in foreign missions for His help. I thought that things were finally coming around to my plan. I was beginning to relax a bit.

I told Karalyn of my plan for the evening and invited her to take a long hot shower while I finished the dinner and set the table. She had only been upstairs a few minutes when I heard the shower start running. It was strange. The shower had a buzzing kind of sound to it. As I walked from the den into the dining room, the buzzing sound became intense. I stood there for a second, as the fog cleared from my brain and a wave of reality filled my head with smoke alarm sounds. Turning to the kitchen, I realized that there should be warning labels on Italian loaf bread that says, "Remove Plastic Bag Before Cooking." My wife says there is one on the bag. Once the bag is on fire, it's hard to tell, though. The one good thing about the fire was that my wife was still in the shower and was absolutely clueless to the slight diversion. I didn't want to ruin the bread by putting out the fire with water. My thought process was working as fast as it could to resolve the problem. At the time it seemed like a great idea to put the fire out with Parmesan cheese, so I sprinkled it generously over the plastic coated bread and watch in amazement as the bread again took on an edible appearance.

Karalyn sat down at her place at the table dressed only in a towel draped across her shoulders. She was ravishing. I was really impressed by her glow. She talked about her day as I tonged a large portion of salad into her bowl. She leaned back against the wall and dimmed the lights. I lit the candles. Dinner was served.

I could not have planned the lighting any better. By the candlelight, my few small indiscretions were hardly noticeable. The soft music and the dinner made both of us real relaxed.

"What is the occasion for all of this?" Karalyn asked innocently.

I told her of my ultimate plan for the evening. Although a little apprehensive of it, Karalyn agreed to the massage under the condition that I not try anything fancy. I was a little hurt by her comments and the fact that she doubted my abilities, but I agreed anyway. After all, I figured after the massage, she would be in a gratefully amorous mood, which was my ultimate goal, anyway.

We agreed to do the dishes later, and with a wink in my direction, Karalyn headed up the steps to our bedroom. I finished putting the food in the refrigerator and started up the steps, too. It was at the last step that I remembered that I needed some massage oil. Our instructor had told us that cooking oil worked best, so I told Karalyn that I would return in a minute and headed back to the kitchen. I looked in the cabinet where the spare bottle of cooking oil magically appears after I finish wasting the original, but to my surprise, one had not appeared. I was in big trouble. Without the oil, I could not do the massage. As fate would have it, I leaned against the deep fat fryer. Once my elbow stopped burning, I realized that the oil I needed was sitting right there all along. It did have a slightly fried odor to it, though.

Not to worry. I just tossed in an air freshener refill and in no time it had a great blueberry essence. I ladled a cup or so into an empty squeeze bottle and headed up the steps to our new massage parlor. I did wonder why the bottle twisted and crinkled as I poured in the oil. I thought briefly of fixing it, but I thought that my efforts in the bedroom were needed at this moment. I could fix the bottle later.

Reaching the top of the stairs, I noticed Karalyn was sitting on the bed staring at the room's new object hidden under the an old blue sheet. I pulled back the coverings to reveal our newly installed massage table. You would hardly believe the look on Karalyn's face. I am certain that squirrels have this look when they are in the middle of the road watching a car approach. I gently herded her to the table and helped her into the arm and leg restraints. Lying on her back, she was ready for the massage of her life.

I quickly reviewed my little acrostic in my head. S-H-O-E, Stroke…um Hammering?…Orbit and Expand. That was it. First, stroke.

I poured a generous amount of the smoldering oil onto my wife's lovely back. At this point, I was extremely glad that I had cinched the arm and leg restraints firmly. She leaped into the air a few feet, carrying the table with her. I'm not sure if it was the lingering burning smell from the plastic lid residue or the spark-like glow from the small bits of home fries that made such a romantic setting, but Karalyn sure was excited. She screamed as she twisted and squirmed. The more I oiled and rubbed, the more she responded. When the tummy was done, I flipped her over and strapped her in again. As the last steaming blob of lubricant hit, I began to hammer it into her shoulder blades with a series of karate chops reaching all the way up to her neck. To my surprise, she let out a yell that would unnerve a banshee. She started rising up and spiraling. I started getting excited myself, because I thought that she was getting into the spirit.

I thought that things were going well until I realized that Karalyn's hair was caught in the ceiling fan. There she was whirling around the room, her arms and legs restrained to the bed. I think that laughing at a person strapped to a table and flying around the room like a giant model airplane is one of the worst kinds of rude. But I couldn't help it. I could see that Karalyn was getting a little upset, but anyone else that had walked into this scene would have laughed, too.

Working the situation through my mind, I realized that the next step was orbit, so I mentally crossed that off the list. After I watched a few more revolutions, I understood that Karalyn was not coming down on her own. I was going to have to get her down. I began to formulate a plan to unhook her from the ceiling fan. At this point, it would have been better to turn the fan off and wait until the fan came to a complete stop before trying to free Karalyn. The look on her face, however, said that my life depended on every second of time. The only plan that came to mind was to cut the hair that was stuck in the spinning fan blades. It seemed like a reasonable plan at the time.

I grabbed the large scissors from the sewing table and positioned myself near the spinning fan and waited for the proper moment. As the table spun across in front of me, I snipped a good size piece of hair, freeing Karalyn. As fate would have it, the table flew through the open door and through the not yet repaired holes that the arms had made earlier. I hollered for Karalyn to stop, but she insisted on sailing out of the upstairs window. She sailed out across the lawn and performed a perfect three point landing. But as good as her landing was, her taxiing left a lot to be desired. Karalyn lifted her head and legs, trying to use them to help guide that plane table. It finally came to rest when it crashed into the neighbor's picnic table. Luckily, the neighbors heard the glass breaking and were able to leave the table before Karalyn's vehicle collided into it.

As you can imagine, I assumed that I was in big trouble. There sat buck naked Karalyn, dripping with cooking oil, strapped spread eagle to a table, sprawled out in front of the neighbors, with a large chunk of her hair missing. My first thoughts were that I could make it to the truck before she got to a gun, but then the neighbors helped her get out of the restraints. I must remember to pay Brother Bill back for that.

There was no way that I was going to get out of this alive, unless there were too many witnesses around. I thought that my best course of action was to carry Karalyn a robe and slippers. As I walked across the lawn, I could see an icy cold stare drift from Karalyn's eyes. In great contrast, I could see that Bill and Dawn were fighting back the largest wave of laughter known to man. As I handed Karalyn the robe and shoes, I could see her face melt into a smile as she leaned against the brick wall of our neighbor's house. This was extremely perplexing to me until a cold chill ran up my back. Looking down, I realized that in all of the commotion, I had forgotten to dress myself.

After a small and more surely not adequate explanation, Karalyn and I made a hasty retreat to our house. For my punishment, I must never practice massage again, and I am forbidden to go to any more auctions, or use a pair of scissors ever again. Too drastic a punishment, I think.

Nudist Among Us

Spring that year seemed more than a little dramatic. The air was a little more yellow with pollen, and the grass was just a shade more green. The tree leaves had finally hidden our house from view of the street. We finally had our privacy, again.

As the first blossoms of spring appear on the lawn, my mind eases back to the verses in Matthew that talk about the lilies of the field being the finest dressing for the earth. When you think about it, the earth is really naked, except for the areas that we have placed asphalt and concrete to enhance our stay here. Think how much prettier the world would be without its clothes.

Spring ushers in a lot of other outdoor activities as well. There are the Easter Egg Hunts, spring cleanings and repairs, and spring trips to the Emergency Room for repairs to the husbands wounded in action. You can almost set your calendar by the increase in prayer requests on the church prayer line. I'm not certain, but I think that is how most church secretaries know to set the clocks forward for Daylight-Saving Time. When the first request for Brother Jim's bad back comes in, it's time to move your clock forward.

The prayer line is the lifeblood of most churches. It is the modern day Town Crier. It delivers to each member of the church an up-to-date account of the latest gossip circulating among the ladies of the church. With just the touch of a finger, you can call up and listen to what is happening to the pastor's daughter, who that hussy divorcee was sitting beside Brother Willie this Sunday, and which church family hosted the covered dish supper last week that resulted in five members coming down with the flu. You can get all of the sordid details from all of the most reliable sources through the modern miracle delivered to us via Ma Bell.

Now, there is one small hurdle that you have to overcome first. You must speak Prayer Line, a language so sneaky and conniving that only a blessed few can understand, and only after many years of intense study. I, myself, have yet to master this language, but I have a working knowledge of its basic functions. I rely on my wife to translate long or complicated statements when the need arises.

As a shining example, let's review last weeks prayer requests. It all begins with the pastor enumerating the usual requests, safe return of missionaries from areas that we can't even pronounce, a few sick people with diseases that I personally don't want to get near, and the ever present slump in the giving last week. Not too hard to understand. He wants you to know that the missions giving and the budget giving is a little slack. He reminds us that if we don't catch up, he is going to ask us to visit the sick people in the hospital with him, subjecting us to all kinds of demonic diseases. You would think that the pastor would want to protect us from these, wouldn't you?

Next, we move into the plight of poor Mrs. Erma's daughter. It seems that the poor girl can't find any dresses that properly fit those long spindly legs of hers. So says her mother. I seem to recall that Mrs. Erma had the same problem with her dresses being way too short when she was courting her husband. It seems that short skirts are hereditary.

Moving on, we find the Johnson brothers with a bit of trouble and in the hospital. It appears that Tom's wife accidentally struck him on the head with a frying pan after his return from a family gathering at "Julia's Mud Wrestling Parlor." His brother Billy is recovering from the same injury received from his wife, also. The church members are glad to know that they are convalescing together in Room 114 at the local hospital.

The last bit of news was my favorite, the winner of the "Grandma Bowl." As strange as it seems, there is always a competition for the last unmarried guy in the church. The married women try desperately to fix him up with the next eligible widow on the list. The eligible widows try desperately to be the next one on the list. I especially like the manner of language that ensues when a winner is declared.

"We wish to rejoice on the quick recovery that has come to our Brother Ray in his hour of grief with the death of his first wife, Clara. He seems to be doing fine now, and asks that the fine ladies of the Senior Singles class cease from sending food and desserts to his house, especially the ones that show up at ten o'clock at night and have forgotten to change from their silk negligees. Sister Evelyn says that there are nights when as many as three women will arrive at that unusual hour of the evening. It is a shame what Ms. Evelyn has seen while caring for our bereaved Brother Ray."

"No explanation is necessary for why Sister Evelyn is at his house at ten o'clock," my wife says with that grand little smirk. "She won."

Whether Brother Ray knew it or not, he had just become the grand prize at a hog tying contest. I find it unique that the language of love and the language of a prayer line are equally confusing. Perhaps it's because they are both the languages of women.

As is our usual routine, my wife, my son, and I headed off for church the next Sunday. My wife was confident of all that was on the prayer line. She had studied earnestly, just in case there was a test. She was ready to take her place in the middle row of the church. As we walked through the doors, the buzzing of gossip filled the air. The ladies were hot on the trail of any detail that might have missed the prayer line. As I wandered aimlessly around the portico among the smoking group of our church, my wife dove head first into the mire that had become "Gossip Central."

I like standing among the smokers. It is as close to the incense burning of the early church as we get in today's worship. I am not sure if God thinks it a worthy, pleasant smell, but it can't hurt. But I…well, you know.

As I stood there, Mrs. Nancy returned to her car to get her cell phone. It became apparent that she had forgotten to check for last minute messages and was grossly behind on the conversation. Standing next to the brilliant red columns that I was leaning on, she gasped slowly at first, and then screamed. I thought perhaps the phone was electrocuting her, so I grabbed the phone and tossed it to the ground. I must admit that I thought that I should have made sure that she had completely released the phone before I threw it to the ground. If not then, at least before I stomped it into submission. I really wondered why the screaming phone sounded exactly like Mrs. Nancy.

As I helped Mrs. Nancy from the ground, she kept muttering something about a new message that came in too late to be heard by most of the group. I wasn't quite sure what she meant, but I was sure that she sincerely wanted her phone back. I was still not convinced that it was not a maniac killer phone, but I figured that Nancy could definitely kill me, so I gave her the phone back.

Over and over, she listened to the message. She stuck her head into the door and motioned for the herd of women in the gossip hall to come over. With all of the ladies congregated around her, she recited word for word the latest prayer line message. Each lady took turns listening to the message, trying to pick up on the voice in the message, but to no avail.

As Karalyn and I meandered to our Sunday School class, she briefed me on the message that was on the prayer line, there was a nudist among us. This was hardly news to the two of us, but it seemed to upset Karalyn to no end. I guess she was afraid that whoever knew this was going to reveal the names, and we would be ostracized from the church. Frankly, if I had thought that we could be kicked out of the jobs at the church and be allowed to attend without the forced labor, I would have taken out an ad in the bulletin and placed a billboard on the front lawn years ago.

The members of our class were still milling around talking when we came in the room. Much to Karalyn's surprise, there were no lynching parties waiting, and we were not stripped of our rank in the church. She leaned over to me and whispered that things were going well so far. I told her that they were probably waiting until our tithe check cleared to attack. She was not amused.

I noticed that Brother Ray was next to the piano talking with Mrs. Rosalyn, one of the Grandma Bowl contestants. Obviously, she was the runner up and would serve in the place of Sister Evelyn should she not be able to complete her term. I could only imagine what ills could befall the winner that would allow the runner up to take her place.

Brother Ray talked a while and shuffled over to his usual seat. Mrs. Rosalyn followed. The whole time, Mrs. Evelyn was watching the discussion out of the corner of her eye. She could see that the only chair next to Brother Ray was the chair that Mrs. Rosalyn was heading for. Not wanting to give any ground to her new prize, Mrs. Evelyn moved to stake her claim on that chair.

Anyone that has not seen a foot race between two seventy-year-old ladies has really missed something. Mrs. Rosalyn had the speed, but she was still no match for Mrs. Evelyn's crafty style. As the two neared the corner at the piano, Mrs. Evelyn jerked Mrs. Rosalyn's walker, wedging it between the chalkboard and the door. Mrs. Rosalyn fell into the row of chairs and sprawled across the floor. Mrs. Evelyn should be given an Academy Award for the sympathy act that she performed as Mrs. Rosalyn rolled around on the floor. Stretching her arms out, Mrs. Evelyn plopped herself down in the prized seat and feigned a scream of pain. To all but the most cunning people, it looked like a fair race. Of course all of the ladies knew what had happened. Still, for the rest of the Bible study, Mrs. Evelyn kept a death grip on Old Ray's arm.

As is the custom in our class, the end of the session is for review of the prayer requests and a listing of the praises. Janice started with the Johnson brothers drinking and womanizing. Just in case none of the other guys got the message, each wife prayed that God would give them the just reward that they deserved. Personally, I felt that the frying pan may have been a little harsh, but then some ladies were advocating public castration. Even the moderate wives were issuing rolling pins and large skillets to the newly married women of the church, just in case their husbands might need a little reminder once in a while.

Next, we covered Ms. Erma's daughter, and then to poor Old Brother Ray. We were rounding out the last of the prayer concerns and praises when Mrs. Rosalyn started to convulse. She was shaking and trembling like there was something inside of her about to explode. Her arms started flailing and waving so as to cause all manners of commotions. Just when I thought that she would explode, the words came bursting out of her mouth. "Ain't we gonna pray for the pervert nudist?"

The room went deafly quiet. No one moved for almost a second. The words hung in mid air, then slowly settled to the ground like a leaf. Janice leaned forward, still shocked, and asked, "What nudist?"

Mrs. Rosalyn settled back in her chair, proud to be the first to bring it up the calamity. She clinched her pocketbook to her chest and announced that there were nudists among us. All around us. They said so on the prayer line. It must be so.

Janice tried to convince Mrs. Rosalyn that someone must be joking, but that was not possible. Once something is on the prayer line, it is as good as gospel. Janice finally relented and asked that we pray for the nudies.

The car ride home from church that afternoon was less than joyful. I know that St. James cautions us to consider it great joy to be in the midst of tribulation, but then, St. James never had to ride home in the van with my wife. It wasn't one of those screaming, "how could you do this," type of arguments. It was more like a silent siege. No one talked. When we turned into the driveway, my son did a rolling exit from the car and got as far away from us as possible. Smart move for a boy of eleven. He will survive just fine as a husband some day. I have trained him well.

Upon entering the house, I walked to the bedroom, tossing my jacket on the bed, my shirt on the floor, and my pants over the ringing telephone. After answering the phone, my wife hung my coat in the closet, threw my shirt and pants into the hamper just before stubbing her toe on my boots that lay beside the bathroom door. From the screams that emitted from the bedroom, I was surely glad that I had made my way downstairs and was reclining in my favorite chair.

There is one really good thing about a man's recliner. It is like his own country. You can lay there unharmed by the goings on around you. You have this invisible force field around you that protects you. It makes you invisible to the rest of the world. It is our harbor in any storm. I try to stay near it as much as possible.

On this particular day, the chair probably saved my life. There was a steady stream of calls from the ladies of the church, all seeking to divine the true identity of the nudists in our church. First, it was Mrs. Shirley, calling to say that it was certainly not the Jones, as they were just too short to be nudists. Nor could it be the Horners; they were too fat. The Smiths were just too ugly.

The next call came from our deacon, saying that he had informed the pastor that it was not any of his flock but that he wanted to know if there was anything that we wanted to confess before he made such a reasonable statement. My wife said that there was nothing in this world that she wanted to confess anywhere near the prayer line or the pastor. Truer statements were never made.

Shortly after dinner, Karalyn sat in the Florida room with me, holding her toe and contemplating the day's events. With each ring, she had faced the lion and had survived. With night drawing near and dead tired from the fight, she laid her head on my shoulder and drifted into a somber haze. All had quieted. I sat watching television and wondering what it would be like to disclose the wonderful feeling of clothes free worship to my church.

The phone rang again. I told Karalyn not to get up and I would get it. Then I realized that she was lying in my lap. I probably should have figured this out when I saw her head bob as I stood up. I really came to grips with the extent of the problem when I saw Karalyn's head bounding off of the coffee table.

Luckily for her, the floor broke her fall.

I reached the phone in time to hear the pastor's voice on the other end. He asked for Karalyn, and feeling relieved, I gave her the phone. I returned to my chair to finish the baseball game.

I could hear the distinct sound of my wife bounding toward the Florida Room. I peered out of the edge of my eye at her as she stood in the doorway, holding her head and seething anger out of every pore.

I knew that the best course of action for me was to either play dead or pretend to be asleep. Since my portrayal of both is pretty much the same, I went forward with my plan. It wasn't until she asked if I was asleep that I knew which course I would take. I think that the most convincing part of my act was the fake snoring. I had argued on many occasions that I do not snore, thus providing me the best evidence of sleep.

Karalyn shrugged her shoulders and snorted a small fireball from her nostril as she left me in search of the next male available. I felt bad for my son, but it was survival of the fittest. I had trained him well and had given him the necessary knowledge to escape the tyranny. What he did next was up to him.

Just before he was devoured, the phone rang again.

"Hi, Pastor," Karalyn said. "Good to hear from you again."

A long pause was followed by, "Did we do what? Hold on, please."

Karalyn placed her hand over the phone and motioned for me to come over. Feeling like the sleep thing was still working, I laid motionless. I can't be sure if there was an earthquake or if Karalyn grabbed the world by the tail and shook it, but I landed next to her with the phone in my hand.

"Good afternoon, Pastor."

He responded that he just wanted to hear what my voice

sounded like on the phone. He cordially reminded me that getting people worked up with a practical joke was, to say the least, childish.

As his voice died into a dial tone, I realized that in a few minutes the church would return to normal. I sat in my chair, pretending to be awake and wondering what the next prayer line message might be. The evening mellowed into the night. Before going to bed, I reached for the phone and dialed the number to the prayer line. I listened intently as the pastor relayed the newest church happenings.

"Today, we grieve with Mrs. Sadie, as her pet pig has run away from home. On a similar note, we would like to give a special praise for those lovely hams, pork ribs, and Boston butts that Mr. Chester and Mrs. Karalyn brought to the church barbeque and social time last week," the pastor said in a quivering voice, gulping profusely. I guess that I will be getting a call shortly from the pastor again.

A New Church for Us

"I think that you could further the Lord's ministry by joining another church," our pastor said with a calm demeanor. "Perhaps the Muslims would be more to your liking."

Now, I've heard of stealing members from other churches, before. I have heard of converting people of other beliefs. I think that this is the first time that I have heard of a pastor trying to convert a member to another faith. I thought about his proposition for a little while. I considered the possibilities and the advantages. I still thought that I had the best deal, so I decided against it.

"I was afraid you would say that," the pastor mumbled under his breath.

I knew that this situation had come from a small incident during the Lord's Supper where I inadvertently bumped the pastor in the head with the tray of small grape juice glasses. The cut wasn't large for the amount of blood that gushed forward. Nor was the carpet that new. I really didn't see what all the fuss was about. The event seemed pretty funny to me. Pastor looked more like a murder victim that the anything else. I guess the chalk outline around his unconscious body was just a little too much. But I digress.

It just seemed that the pastor was in need of a break from us. God laid on our heart that it was time for us to seek another place of worship before the pastor had to be committed to an institution. So, with the fervor of a sack full of potatoes, we ventured out into the world to find a church in need of our special talents.

Old Time Gospel Hour

The first church that we decided to visit was a small country church just around the corner from us. It was an old, unpainted clapboard building nestled among a small grove of oaks. As we walked from the parking lot to the church, I kept replaying the old time gospel songs in my mind. I could never remember if it was the little brown church or little brown jug in the wild wood. From the appearance of the congregation, it didn't seem to matter much.

We sat down at the first available wooden pew in the front of the church. Sitting next to us was the pastor's wife and their children, two daughters and a son. The church was a small one room building with large narrow windows. The old, upright, out of tune piano sat in the corner next to the rack with all the choir robes. As we shifted and moved on the pews, the creaking could be heard in the parking lot.

When the piano had been playing for a while, the pastor stepped to the podium and bellowed the sermon in a lyrical country drawl. He preached on heaven for a minute, then on hell for the rest of the week that we spent there that day. Each time I thought that he was slowing down, someone from the back would holler, "Preach on!"

Now, I figure if the Lord wanted him to preach on, it was not my place to say anything. But if the Lord wanted it, He didn't need any help in conveying the message. So, when the pastor started to slow down the next time, I stood up and hollered, "Amen, Pastor. That says it all."

My wife used the international sign for stop talking. She elbowed me in the ribs. Not wanting to stand out or be conspicuous, I slumped back down on the pew.

The pastor took the hint and began to wind down into the alter call. He offered an invitation for anyone that wanted to join the church to move into the aisles and come on down as the band played. I looked around to see where they had hid and entire band in a one room building. There in the corner, next to a few old tomato crates, was a guitar player, banjo picker and a fiddler.

For a group of squatty old fellas with Civil War surplus instruments, they sure could lay down the sound. The trio began with a droning rendition of *The Old Rugged Cross*. They picked up the tempo with *I Saw the Light*, and reached ramming speed with *I'll Fly Away*.

As the music began to meld into the voices of the congregation, the pastor's son wandered over to me. Standing there, he tugged gently on my pants leg. I asked him what he wanted with a curious smile.

"Mister, do you know how to handle a snake?" he asked politely.

I thought it was a strange question to ask at this moment, but I figured that he was just a bored as I was. So, with a big smile, I answered, "Of course I do."

With that, the boy ran to the back of the church next to the tomato crates. I returned to the song and began singing again. I was just about completely engulfed by the music when I felt another tug on my leg. Turning, I could see out of the corner of my eye that the boy had pulled one of the crates over next to me and was prying open the lid.

The pastor announced to the congregation that one of our visitors felt moved by the spirit. I was excited to see a response to the sermon, but I had thought that we were the only visitors that day, and neither my wife nor my son seemed to be moving toward the front of the church. I wondered who the visitor was.

A third tug on my pant leg gleaned a stilted response to the young fellow. I turned to address the now annoying child just in time to see the small boy pull a huge snake from the crate and hand it in my direction.

Now, there are many things that you can hand over to me. You can hand me money. You can hand me cakes and pies of many flavors, but a angle headed buck-toothed slithering snake is awfully low on the list.

In the same vein, it is a poor idea to even show my wife a snake. She is not the sort to take kindly to any snake, poisonous or not. She let out a Rebel Yell that scared the dead confederate soldiers buried in the graveyard out back.

The young lad looked at me with a sheepish grin while reminding me that I had said that I could handle a snake. I reached into my vest pocket and retrieved my Sunday and Go to Meeting pistol and fired two rounds into the snakes head. I blew the smoke from the end of the barrel and placed the derringer back in my vest pocket. The meeting came to screeching halt.

The boy reeled in fright. I turned to him and said, "There, it's handled."

The pastor looked over in the direction of the blast, spying his trembling son holding a limp, lifeless snake over the boy's arm. The look on the pastor's face said it all.

As we exited the door of the church, the pastor shook our hands and told us of a wonderful church down the street that really could use our help. My wife smiled and departed in a full sprint toward the car. So much for the Full Gospel Independent Primitive Bible Preaching Baptist Conservative Movement Apostolic Brethren Of Southern Rock Hollow – like there was more that one in Rock Hollow.

Liturgy

The week came and went. The sun rose each day and set each night, just as it had done for years. Each evening on the porch, Karalyn and I would study on which church to try next. I wanted to go to "The Living Church" on Trader Road. It had a great big cross in the front yard and a big billboard for a fence around the play ground. Karalyn wanted the visit the Liturgical church down the street. Searching my brain for clues that might make the best choice, I kept coming back to the small nagging voice in the back of my head that said, "Listen to your wife." I relented and agreed that this might be the best place to visit. Later, I found out that the voice I heard was Karalyn standing behind me chanting, "Listen to your wife." I think that she thought that there was no way for anything to go wrong there. The services had been the same for centuries, and no amount of input from us could alter the course. My wife is usually much brighter than that.

We sat in the pews in the center of the church. I tried to sit in the center of the row so as to be perfectly aligned with the pastor. As the music began, one of the pastors came walking down the aisle shaking a box from side to side. As he passed, I realized that the reason he was shaking the box was because it was on fire. Smoke was pouring out from the box and filling the sanctuary with a thick dark smell. Thinking quickly, I leaped over the people next to us and knocked the box from the pastor's hand. I hollered, "Don't worry, Preacher. I got it." It didn't seem to calm him, though.

I emptied the box on the carpet and began to stomp out the embers. I am not sure what was so important as to make such a fancy box, but whatever it was, it was gone now. There was nothing left of the treasure that the fancy box stored except some old sooty ashes that I had ground into the carpet.

The pastor must have really cherished those items because he became angry when he saw the carpet and what remained of the box. He stormed out of the church screaming something in Latin. The service was cancelled.

While leaving the service, I asked the other pastor what the other one said. Roughly translated, the good father had bid us good church hunting in the protestant movement.

We next visited the Presbyterian church down the road. As we parked in the lot, I noticed a buzz among the congregation. Apparently, someone had noticed that we were visiting them. Boy, did I feel impressed that the entire deacon board, the pastor, and the men's ministry came out to greet us.

As we neared the door, the group stopped our progress and informed us that their insurance company had instructed them not to let us in. They said that their policy only covered normal accidents, but "professional accident subjects" were not part of a normal church policy. They did, however, offer to buy us lunch at a location of our choice, so long as it was not owned by any of the members. I thought it a fair trade.

Southern Baptist, Born and Bred

"They are coming back, my aching head." *—Pastor Greg*

On Saturday night, my wife came across an ad in the paper about a friendly church with contemporary music and a friendly smile. It was perfect for us. It was, however, our original church.

We made our way to church that Sunday and took our regular seats in the sanctuary. We sat through the service and greeted all of the people we knew. We were back home. As we left the building, the pastor shook our hands and said that he would see next Sunday. I wondered if he still had the stitches under the Band-Aid.

Christian Denomination Sorter

As you can see from the previous adventure, we were having a difficult time deciding just what denomination that fit our family. I felt like others may be struggling with this situation, also. To help with this situation, I have written a foolproof tendency test to help you find the perfect denomination.

Please take a few minutes to fill out the question below, placing the letter of your response in the line provided at the edge.

_____ 1) In Baptism…

a. you prefer to have a sprinkling of water tossed gently on your face.

b. you prefer to be immersed into a warm tub of water.

c. you are so afraid of water that when you come up out of the water, you are screaming and praising God for letting you survive the ordeal.

d. you don't care, so long as you can skinny dip in the baptismal pool while the baptism continues.

_____ 2) In the Ordinance of the Lord's Supper…

a. you feel that elements are the body and blood of Christ.

b. you feel that the elements are representative of the body and blood of Christ.
c. you start screaming and shouting to the heavens when that dry miniature cracker gets lodged in your throat, then praise God when the grape juice washes it clean.
d. you ask for seconds. You also can't figure out why they think a plate full of crackers and glass full of wine divided among so many people is considered a feast.

_____ 3) The only good snakes are…
a. the ones formed from Moses's staff.
b. the dead ones.
c. the ones that put themselves back in the cage by themselves while the congregation dines on cyanide coffee and rat poison cheesecake.
d. barbequed over real hot coals and basted with balsam oil, garlic and oregano.

_____ 4) Singing in the Sunday service should be…
a. kept to a bare minimum.
b. joyful and lighthearted.
c. come right after the faith healing and during all three offering collections.
d. be accompanied by drums, guitars, and go-go dancers. Requests should be granted for any donation over 50 cents.

_____ 5) When the offering plate is passed, you…
a. go to the restroom until it passes on through.
b. roll out a crisp new five dollar bill.
c. roll out a crisp five dollar bill for you and each of your children.
d. roll out a crisp one dollar bill, pick your teeth with it, throw it in the offering plate, but take out four one's and four quarters.

_____ 6) When it comes to recognizable objects in the church, the first thing that come to mind is…
a. the crucifix.
b. the pulpit.
c. the casserole dish.
d. the back row.

_____ 7) At social gatherings of the church, you prefer…
a. finger foods and good wine.
b. pot luck casseroles and good conversation.
c. fried chicken, coleslaw, biscuits with red-eye gravy, beans of every description, and every dessert known to man. If its bad for you, bring it on. Sweet tea to drink.
d. whatever the Baptist Church down the street left in the kitchen unattended during the service.

_____ 8) Alcohol is…
a. a perfectly acceptable drink so long as you drink it in moderation.
b. can't be drunk when the pastor is around.

c. used to light the flames for baptism by fire when we slay someone in the spirit.
d. more than just a drink. You can clean with it and run your car on it.

_____ 9) My body is…

a. the life support system for my eternal soul.
b. a temple dedicated to God.
c. thrown about brutally when the Spirit hits me.
d. a sexual funhouse for any willing partner of the opposite sex.

_____ 10) When I die…

a. my soul will be judged by a merciful God.
b. I'll go directly to heaven.
c. there will be dancing in the street, parties everywhere, and a feast of epic proportions.
d. I'll use my "Get Out of Hell Free" card that I bought from that preacher on TV.

Now that you have completed the questions, add up the total number of a's, b's, c's and d's. Refer to the chart below to find the church that most closely represents your style of worship.

If you had a majority of a's, then…
your style of worship is more refined and observing the finer graces in life. The Catholic, Episcopal, and Lutheran churches are good choices. They are more quiet, stilted, stiff and stuffy. That should suit you fine.

If you have more b's, then…

your style of worship is more casual. You are a blue jeans and t-shirt sort of person, a real blue collar type, the backbone of America. You are more relaxed in your worship. You just sit there slouched over the pew and sleep through the pastor's sermon. The Baptist and Methodist church would be your best choice.

If you have more c's, then…

your style of worship fits the Pentecostal movement well. Just install your earplugs and head off to the nearest Primitive Baptist, Holiness, or Church of the Divine Right Movement and enjoy the frolics of the afternoon. Bring a good appetite and plan to stay all day. Services start at sunrise.

If you have more d's, then…

you've got more problems than one denomination can fix. Even the ecumenical churches don't want you and The Satanist Society said that you will give them a bad name. But as a way of repairing this, we are putting such people on an "assigned risk" waiver and parceling them out to the various churches. Please wait for your assignment before attending another service.

Happy Trail Campers

On the occasion that my wife and I get to escape for a weekend, we usually pick a nudist place near us to camp. We pack all of our belongings in the camper and truck and head out for fun and frolic in the sun. Well, not every time. Lately, it has been more of heading out for a freeze and shiver in the cold damp camper to watch it rain. But I digress.

This past weekend, we headed north and spent a weekend with some wonderful friends while revisiting the comforts of a nudist association we visited last fall. The plan was to see what the place was like in the warmer time and to meet the regulars. Karalyn and I had taken the club tour at a previous visit several months ago and were talking about the possibilities of joining the club. Actually, I was talking about wanting to join the club. Karalyn was wanting to know what the club was like when the weather was good.

Our plan was to leave promptly at noon. We, of course, left promptly at 3:39 p.m.. We headed north, packed in my pick-up truck so tight that any movement of the people on the passenger side would cause the driver to flinch, sending the truck and camper into oncoming traffic. Combining this level of comfort with the thrill and suspense of an amusement park ride is less difficult when you add the element of torrential rains and suicidal drivers. Clearly, so long as we thought that we were on a Disney Land ride, the family could endure the trip.

We sped along Interstate 95 heading toward Washington at the speed of light – as long as you can accept the speed of light at 25 mph. We dodged this car and that car. We wove in and out of oncoming traffic. Playing bumper cars with the traffic seemed to be my personal favorite part of the trip. My son's favorite part was when I decided that there was no need to stop breathing while drinking a Pepsi.

I had concluded that, since there was carbonation in the drink and that carbonation had oxygen in it, the lungs should be able to process the Pepsi just like air. Therefore, there was no need to stop the breathing process just to take a small sip of Pepsi. I took a long pull on the Pepsi bottle and continued to breathe as before. I am sure that at some time in my life someone had told me of the dangers of breathing while drinking, but it was not until I noticed that the lungs really don't like Pepsi that these little informational gems became to be important to me.

I coughed. I choked. I turned a beautiful shade of Petty blue. I'm not much of a Petty fan, but I understand that it matched my shirt perfectly, until the point that I coughed an entire mouthful of Pepsi on it. The dashboard, being gray, also clashed with the Pepsi. My wife, the fashion expert, had to clean that up immediately so as not to offend the rescue squad should I not survive my little breathing experiment. I am certain that the car that we ran off the road agreed with her decision because they started honking the horn and waving the "You're no. 1" finger at us. Thinking that every good gesture should be acknowledged in kind, I returned the praise.

It seemed that the trip was progressing well. In fact, we completed the two and a half hour trip in just over four and a half hours. This was a personal family best. Richard Petty would be proud.

Arriving at the club, we rang the little buzzer at the gate that lets the person in the office know that a customer has finally arrived. This system presupposes that the person whose job it is to answer the buzzer is seated in her chair by the intercom and is responsive to the buzzer when it rings. This, having failed, reverted us to the stand-by system, which seemed to be that you stand by the gate in the pouring rain until a member of the club passes by and opens the gate.

I drove up to the office and walked in, announcing our arrival in as majestic a voice as I could summon. The kind lady behind the desk began searching for our reservations on the computer. I began to think that perhaps the reservation system was different in this state than in Virginia. It seems that the system here only tracks the fact that you are coming and not the particulars of your stay. We were routed to a tent site that was a lovely grass space in which to drive our 5-ton unit. Unfortunately, under that pretty grass was some very ugly mud.

Not wanting to be discouraged by this, or by the downpour of rain, I looked around to see just who exactly was supposed to go out and set up the campsite. It became apparent from the cold stares that I was receiving that I was the responsible for this task. I opened the door to the truck and began giving assembly orders to the other members of the family. I just figured if I led the way that they would follow. This time the plan worked.

I assigned the water line connection to my wife and the electrical connection to my son. I took on the task of unhooking the trailer hitch and sway bars. As I rounded the corner, carrying the metal bars and jack, I noticed my son standing in the rain staring at the electrical outlet. I shouted to him not to worry about the rain in the outlet, that I was sure that the plugs were grounded. Besides, he looks really good with frizzy hair.

The problem seemed to be that the plug didn't fit. Ajay tried every conceivable position to plug that dang thing in, but to no avail. Finally, he requested the presence of an adult at the location. He did this, of course, by throwing the electrical cord into the ever growing water puddle. Seeing that Ajay needed help, I began to shout great pearls of wisdom in his direction, causing the neighboring campers to close their windows.

I sauntered over to the electrical outlet, only to find that my son was correct, the plug didn't fit the outlet. My first thought was to buy an adapter that would allow us to hook up to a regular wall outlet, and we would soon be in business. When I saw my son sauntering back from the camp store empty handed, I realized that we had to move the camper.

I sent my wife to the store to inform the staff that we had to move to another location that would have the proper electrical connections. I selected site number six. I busied myself re-hooking the trailer and backing it into space number six. I watched with special affection as my wife thrashed her arms violently in the air when I connected the last piece of the trailer to the site. Apparently, someone else had reserved that site before us, and we had to leave this place, also.

It takes the greatest amount of character to withstand the final straw landing on the camel's back and not explode. I felt fairly proud of myself for not becoming an axe murderer up to this point. I even felt that my chances were fairly good for surviving a sanity, hearing once we found the next best site, "Number A." Does anyone else feel a little foreshadow from a place that is numbered with a letter?

I hooked the trailer to the truck once again and made my way to good ole site "Number A" and proceeded to back the trailer into place. Jumping from the truck, I realized that the rain had reached the torrent level, and the winds were almost to gale force. I thought how fortunate we were to have this particular weekend to vacation in a resort campground.

Shouting orders like a true camp slave master, I instructed

everyone to forge forward and quickly complete the task of setting up the trailer. I began unhooking the truck, and manhandled the electrical cable over to the hookup. Defiantly, the cable fought to remain next to the trailer, but my brute strength allowed me to force the five-pound cable into submission. The connection at the outlet, however, beat me. With only a small whimper, I muttered the unthinkable, "a fifty amp connection."

Yes, that's right! The wrong connector again. I screamed in as polite a manner as I could for my wife to ask the store operator if he had a thirty to fifty-amp adapter. Being the loving and obedient wife that she is, she trotted off to the store once again. Returning a few minutes later, she announced that all they had was a fifty-amp to a thirty-amp adapter.

I am not certain just how calm I was explaining to her that they were the same thing, but apparently it was not calm enough to convince her to retrieve the adapter. I went to the store myself and bought the adapter. Well, almost. I was about half of a buck short of the bill. I left Ajay as collateral. I think that he was relieved when I returned with the fifty-three cents.

Ajay, having learned much from his previous experience hooking up trailers, elected to hook up the garden hose to the water supply, avoiding any possible conflict with the electrical supply. Having reviewed the process, he now admits that this was one of the flaws in his character, that of finding the one task in life with no possible solution. As he dragged the water hose over the water connection, he realized that the hose was just a few feet too short.

I am not certain that anyone not present could fully conceive of the picture of a thirteen-year-old standing just short of a hydrant and not wanting to tell anyone. I guess he thought that we would not notice that the trailer did not have any water until he was a safe distance from us.

Finally, he made the fateful announcement. His eyes were fixed on the rather large skillet that I had in my hands. The strangest look of relief crossed his face as the skillet landed gently on the table between us. I am not sure why.

With nothing else left to do, I went to the store myself to see about buying a garden hose to connect the last utility to our trailer. Finding that there is a strange shortage of garden hoses in this state, the lady offered a wonderful piece of advice. As I asked her about the closest place to find a garden hose, she suggested a High's might be close. Not recognizing that store brand, I asked for information about the it. I also commented that, in our area, High's is an ice cream store. She confirmed that, in her area, they were, too, but they were the closet store to the campground.

Seeing no solution to the problem in the camp store, I ventured to the trailer to convince my wife that we could live without water for a few days, and that all would be well in the morning. Fortunately, the neighbor came to our rescue and lent us a hose.

As we tightened the hose in place, the sky cleared. We all decided to skip dinner for a while, sit in the hot tub, and watch the stars. There is nothing so calming as good conversation with friends while sitting in a nudist hot tub. After a few brief moments of peace, we dressed and headed to a restaurant for dinner. We stopped by High's on the way back, just in case a free garden hose came with any ice cream purchase. No such luck. I ordered a second ice cream, just in case it was a "buy two, get a garden hose free" sale.

A Christmas Eve Story

The summer pastimes are gone, drifting into the evening chill. The vibrant greens of summer have faded to pastel. September has passed, and October is upon us. As fall approaches, my attention turns mostly to the hobbies of fall. I take brisk naps on the couch as I watch the leaves drift to the ground. I jog to the refrigerator between commercials. I take my hobbies seriously. I even find time to hunt on Saturdays.

Hunting is a time-honored sport of kings and paupers. Men have pursued this adventure even before recorded history. It is so ingrained in our programming that most of what men do is based on the principals of hunting. Our very behavior is controlled by the natural instinct to hunt.

The fall wandered into a cold, snowy Christmas Eve, and all of the guys were sitting around the fire at our hunt club's palatial estate. Actually, it's an old school bus with the wheels for a table and a wood stove pipe poking out one of the broken windows. We sat around the fire, telling lies about the last deer we saw.

Johnny was spinning the same old yarn about a phantom white deer that has been roaming around this neck of the woods since dirt was young. We all listened intently to the story, leaning back from the fire to let the story expand as he went along. The more he told the story, the bigger and older the buck got.

When the story had wound down to its usual conclusion of "it was the biggest deer I ever saw," we decided to head back out into the woods for a last minute hunt. I wasn't anxious to rush home to the pile of unassembled Christmas gifts waiting under the tree.

We crunched through the snow as quietly as seven overweight middle-aged men could. As we crossed over the small hill just above the stream, I noticed what seemed to be a herd of bucks lounging around the pond. They were just wandering along the edge of the water. They appeared to be laughing and snorting at each other.

Apparently, the pond was the deer's equivalent of a water cooler, where they all gather to tell stories and talk about last nights game at the meadow. I'm not sure if you really could consider this a coffee break, but that is what it looked like. But I digress.

I motioned to the intrepid group to stop. Charlie stopped. Bob bumped into Charlie, Tom into Bob, and the rest completed the stop maneuver like someone had outfitted them with a pair of worn out car shocks. It surprised the deer so much that they stood and stared. I guess that they had never seen anything like the bunch before, and they just had to see how this would end.

We shouldered our shotguns and commenced to firing. I stood in amazement as the last shot rang out. Not a single deer was hit. Our brave bunch of highly praised, well camouflaged, painted faced hunters had fired a total of twenty-one shots without hitting one single deer.

As much as it surprised me, it really tickled the deer. They began to laugh. I think that I noticed one deer taunting us by waving, pointing, and shaking his antlers at us. But with a flip of their tails, they were off into the woods. Johnny even started some fabricated tale about the two big deer flying over the trees, but none of us believed him.

From all of the years of hunting, I have never witnessed such a display of poor marksmanship in my entire life. All around the spot where the deer were standing the trees were riddled with holes and the ground was filled with lead. I stood there, staring into the abysmal ground when an old man with a scruffy beard and an old red coat came walking out from the bushes zipping his fly.

"Good job there, idiots!" he exclaimed as he approached us.

The old man reached into a rundown old sleigh and pulled out a notebook. Thumbing through the pages with the fury of a wife on the hunt for her wayward husband, he started pointing at each of us and demanding our names. He scurried about screaming and hollering for his black magic marker and demanding that we return his deer.

It finally hit me. We had been shooting at Santa's reindeer. How could we be so cruel as to shoot at his deer? The other thought that I had was that I was surely glad that we missed. I was equally sure that Santa was crossing us off of his Christmas list.

Oh, the pain of it all. First, I had missed the best opportunity for venison stew, then shot at Santa's reindeer, and last, had been taken off the "good" list. This was turning out to be a lousy day.

Santa finally collapsed into a heap leaning against the sleigh. I studied the expression on his face, hoping for a glimmer of relief from our dilemma. Finally, I walked over to him and placed my hand on his shoulder. I apologized as best as I could, considering that we had tried to kill his livestock. Santa just sat there, staring into space. I returned to my spot over by the stump.

As I passed by the sleigh, I could see all of the packages and presents that Santa were in the process of delivering. When I reached the others, I explained to them what my theory was about this old man, and just how much trouble I thought that we had brought upon ourselves.

Johnny spoke up, "That ain't him. Look at his suit. It's old and wrinkled. Surely, if he can buy presents for all the children of the world, he should be able to buy a new suit once on a while."

I thought about it for a few minutes when Santa stepped up to protest.

"I am in my work clothes," he said with a grimace. "Do you wear your new clothes to slide down chimneys in?"

I had to agree with him. If I were to wear my new suit out to work on the chimney, my wife would kill me. Perhaps Mrs. Claus is about the same way.

Santa speculated about our upbringing and about how our parents didn't raise us right before getting around to the problem at hand. His sled was not capable of delivering the presents to all of the children around the world because we had scared off his reindeer. It was at this point that I decided that it was time for me to bid the fine gentleman a fair evening and exit the area as fast as possible.

Santa, of course, had a different idea. He offered a suggestion that I particularly did not think was such a great idea. Pulling a sled was not the way to spend Christmas Eve. But Santa seemed very determined.

After some discussion about how we would accomplish this event, Johnny came up with the greatest idea he ever had. We would each scour our garages for motors and transmissions and such and convert Santa's sleigh into a motorized vehicle. Santa seemed to warm up to the idea of modernizing his delivery system, mumbling something about not having to deal with the reindeer local anymore, and mentioned how less complicated life had gotten after modernizing the factory to get rid of the Nazi-style elves that used to build his toys. Santa agreed to the deal. He even agreed to restore our names on the "good" list if we were able to deliver the sleigh in time to make the trip by dawn.

After a little discussion, it was determined that my garage was the closet, so we hastily dragged the sleigh to my house. I jacked the front end up and proceeded to cut the single tree and reigns bracket off with the cutting torch. The rest of the guys went scurrying to their homes to scavenge the rest of the stuff from what ever location that they could find.

Tommy was the first to arrive, carrying a transmission. It was a Nash five speed with a twin disc clutch. After a little welding and some hammering on the chassis, the tranny slipped in for a perfect fit.

Tommy and I stood by the door watching patiently when Johnny came staggering through the door. In his right hand was a fuel cell and all of the plumbing necessary to send the petrol rushing toward the engine. In his left hand was half empty jug of moonshine. I suppose that it was full when he began his trip here, but circumstances seemed to dictate that he sample the alcohol before giving it a go in the sleigh. Well, that was his story, anyway.

The next to arrive was Chuck, carrying the rear end and shocks for the back of our newest contraption. He threw them in the pile next to the fuel cell and sampled the jug once, just for luck. I had just finished welding in the brackets for the fuel cell when Chuck shoved the rear into place. After a blood curdling scream, Chuck pulled the rear back enough so that my foot was no longer stuck in Santa's rear end. With a few more choice words as to what I thought could fit inside Chuck's rear, we went back to work.

My wife came bounding out to the garage to see what this fine group of young men were doing and to see if we were going to be in need of bail money. After a small conversation, she informed us that Billy had called, and he was having a hard time securing a front end for the sleigh because his wife was watching her car like a hawk. My wife mentioned something about not touching her van, but it was already too late. Chuck and Johnny had already taken the torches to the front end and were using the tractor to drag it over to the sleigh. I figured at that point I was already sleeping on the couch for the evening, so I welded it in place. It was her fault anyway; she shouldn't have told Chuck about the front end without standing guard over her own.

The sleigh was starting to take shape. All that was left was the motor. We discussed the motor, and I was extremely glad to find out that my wife and I would not be donating to this part of the project. To his credit, Juan was forthright and generous with his offer to allow us to use the motor from his race car. I just hope that he is in the same frame of mind in the spring when he realizes that he donated the motor. A few welds here and there and the motor mounts were in place. We figured that since Juan had already donated the motor, his wife would probably want to donate the exhaust system, too. So, we snatched it from under her '57 Chevy, along with the spring headed dog from the back window.

With all of this in place, we realized that the jug had run empty and that there was not enough to fill a lighter, much less a gas guzzling big block engine. We had to make the trip to Crazy Man Wheller for a refill. I grabbed a five gallon gas can, and Johnny grabbed the jug. We pulled into Crazy Man's house and knocked on the door. One note here, never knock on a moonshiner's house at three o'clock in the morning. They think that you are the Revenuers and start shooting.

After the small commotion ended, I explained the whole

ordeal to Crazy Man. That was the first time that I had ever seen a moonshiner refuse to sell someone liquor. I've seen them sell to children so small that they couldn't hold an I.D., much less possess one. I've seen them sell to pregnant women, to crippled and crazy people. So, when he suggested that this stuff had finally made us crazy, I had to take stock of what was happening. After much haggling and bartering, Tommy finally promised to put Crazy's logo on the back of Santa's sleigh, and we left with the gas can and Johnny's jug full to the brim. Crazy Man also promised to refill the jug should Santa do a personal appearance next Christmas.

Returning to the garage, we finished the project, adding a few minor items to make the sleigh a little more "trick." We added mag wheels and fat tires. We added traction bars and spinner hubs. We added a Hurst shifter and a tach. The wheelie bars and roll cage may have been a little extravagant, but they made the sleigh look so good that we added some shag pile carpet. We topped it off with a killer stereo and matched speakers.

When Santa arrived, he was impressed. After a few warm ups and a couple of burnouts in the driveway, he waved goodby and wished us a Merry Christmas.

A few months later, we got a thank you card from Santa and a package of fruit cakes. We also got a death threat from the Reindeer Local 12-25.

Flying Again

"My Dear Aunt Sally!" I screamed as we collided in the hallway. I was too busy sorting underwear to notice that my wife was carrying my suit to the car when we passed each other. Now our underwear was scattered down the hallway with no way to tell mine from hers. All I could think about was having the plane crash and the rescue people finding out that I had mistakenly worn my wife's lacy panties instead of my manly boxers.

Oh yeah, that's how I tell them apart, I thought. *Her's are more frilly. And smaller. And pink.*

I collected enough panties and boxers to make the two day trip to Wisconsin and slammed them into the suitcase. I reached into my sock drawer and grabbed a handful of white tube socks, adding them to the growing collage of clothing. I grabbed a t-shirt and a spare collared golf shirt and threw them in the suitcase. Last, I got a fresh pair of blue jeans from the dryer and completed my packing.

I noticed that there was plenty of space left in the suitcase for my wife's stuff, so I started adding her items as well. I reached down into the pile of underwear and threw in the pink ones. I reached over into her underwear drawer and got out the blue open cup bra and matching thong panties set that I had bought her for Christmas. Moving down to her nightie drawer, I retrieved the black silk teddy that I got her for her birthday and a pair of fuzzy toe slippers. I topped them off with a pair of purple shorts and a yellow tube top for the ride home. Tossing these into the suitcase, I closed the lid and fastened the locks.

At last, she was finally going to get some use out of the Fred's of Hollywood attire that I had bought her several years ago. Her grandmother's funeral were the perfect place to take these. They matched the new dress that she bought and was perfect fit in the space that I allowed her in the suitcase. I even remembered to bring along a pair of scissors to remove the tags.

As I was heading down the stairs, past the repaired sheet rock from the massage "incident," I felt a strange eerie burning in the back of my neck. It was as if two laser beams were drilling a hole in the back of my head. Fortunately, it was just my wife using her telekinetic power to stop me from loading the suitcase in the car.

"Honey?" she said with a calm demeanor. "I need to pack my stuff in the suitcase before we load it in the car."

With a smile, I reported that the task was already complete and that I had arranged everything for her. She needn't worry. All of her needs were taken care of.

Karalyn took the suitcase back to the bedroom and began to rummage though my clothing selection. She had that special look in her eyes that says that I am in trouble. I wasn't sure what I had done, but I was convinced that in the next few seconds, Karalyn would enumerate each and every single fault that I had ever had.

Sure enough, she did. She began by telling me that the blue bra and pantie set was not appropriate for a funeral. I am not sure who the underwear police are that determined that women can't wear special stuff to a funeral, but I think that it is silly to make such rules.

"The shorts set with the tube top went out of style for me when I developed a chest," Karalyn exclaimed at the top of her abundant voice. "They haven't fit since I married you."

Now, I am not sure that this is so. I distinctly remember her wearing this outfit, and I remember liking her in these clothes at the time. I thought that we were married at that point, but since we have been married for eighteen years, it is hard for me to remember back that far. Seeing her standing next to the shorts set, they did look a little small. I did, however, wonder why she had kept them if they were not the right size anymore and out of style. I thought this as I moved my leisure suit out of my way and returned the shorts set to my wife's drawers.

I sat on the couch patiently while she packed some of the same old stuffy clothing that she wears every day. She did leave the black teddy in the suitcase, but replaced the fuzzy slippers with a pair of rainbow colored toe socks.

Finally, I was ready to load the suitcase into the car and to speed on our way to the airport. We sped toward the airport like a gazelle running from a lion, screaming and snorting. Entering the parking lot, I reached into my pocket for a five-dollar bill to pay for the parking. Karalyn insisted that we didn't pay until we leave, but I was certain that no person would allow you to park without paying for the privilege first. I drove up to the attendant booth and handed the toll lady my money. The kind attendant handed me a ticket and said that I would pay when we leave. I am certain that there was a big smirk on Karalyn's face, but I was not about to look over at her and give her the satisfaction of being right. I had determined that if I didn't look at her, I wasn't wrong. Thus, if I don't look, she can't gloat.

Ever wonder how devious a wife can be? As I avoided looking at her, she reached out and pinched my arm. My natural instinct took over and forced my head to turn and my eyes to focus in on her gloating sneer. She won again.

Now, I am not the best passenger in a car. I don't like to just ride. I feel helpless and alone. I tend to complain a lot. Imagine what it must be like to fly with me. As we entered into the airport, the fellow at the ticket counter took our bag and handed us our tickets. We headed to the gate and passed through the various scanners metal detectors and x-ray machines. I was happy to learn that the x-rays revealed no cavities in my teeth or broken bones in my body.

When we arrived at the waiting area, I started to look around at the passengers that I would be sharing the flight with. I noticed that all of them looked like normal, average terrorists to me. The first one looked like an Arab Muslim terrorist. In fact they all looked that way, including the Chinese lady in the kimono. I was certain that she was a Muslim terrorist, but Karalyn again disagreed with me. Thinking back to the last disagreement with Karalyn, I agreed to get on the plane and fly to Chicago.

I decided that sitting near the window was the best location for me. If the plane started to fall from the sky, I could shove my arms out of the windows and flap my arms wildly. That way I could help the pilot in his hour of need. As I was looking at the window to see how it opened, I noticed a couple of guys in a dented old rusty station wagon pull up to the front of the plane. This didn't concern me until one of them jumped out of the car and hooked a pair of jumper cables to the plane. With a cough and a sputter, the jet engines soon roared to life. I decided to change seats with my wife.

We taxied down the runway and began to start our takeoff. I closed my eyes and pretended that we were just traveling down the interstate to our favorite nudist park. As fear and panic started to set in, I decided to think of safer things, such as walking through the middle of a demolition derby. As the plane lifted off of the ground, my stomach settled nicely around my ankles. I had never thought of storing my stomach there, but it seemed like a handy place at the time, so I left it there.

As we cleared the last of the clouds and leveled off at some grand number of feet in the air, I released my death grip from my wife's hand and began to relax in my chair. I think that the pilot could save us all so much fear and panic if he would just say that we are up in the air and dispense with the report on just how high we are. Personally, I think that he was just bragging.

Turbulence in the air is God's special way of saying to us that he does not want us to fly. I am sure that every time some person launches a plane in the air, God tosses a coin to decide if it will be a smooth flight or if He wants someone to pay for invading His beautiful atmosphere. Today was no exception.

Now, intellectually I know that the little bumps in the sky are just some small air pockets meeting each other. Some warm and some cold, the difference in temperature causes the air to toss the plane slightly. Emotionally, however, I believe that God has placed these massive speed bumps in our path to remind us that, at any moment, He can effect our lives. Personally, I would much rather have a dove drift down on my shoulder and sing a lovely melody of reminder. But I digress.

The sky was certainly alive with small speed bumps. First, we bumped left, and then we bumped right. The flight attendant dribbled the beverage cart past us and on to the front. She seemed like a pleasant lady, polite and kind. She even apologized for spilling the hot coffee over my head. She also apologized for landing the cart in my lap while simultaneously lap dancing with me. She apologized to my wife, though it hardly seemed necessary. Karalyn barely noticed the dance, and since the attendant had begun to give Karalyn a Pepsi shampoo for her inconvenience, I felt that Karalyn had been amply compensated for trouble.

When we crossed over the mountains, our trip became calm. The plane ride was as smooth as glass. I was able to lie back in the chair and shiver at a minimal rate. I even was able to remove most of my fingernails from the arm of the seat. I thought briefly about removing my seat belt, but decided that one small concession to my fears wasn't so bad.

My wife, being made partially of springs and super balls, was bouncing out of her seat and into the aisles. First, she wanted a magazine. Then she needed to go to the ladies' room. Next she needed a drink. Then, it was back to the ladies' room. If it hadn't been for the captain forcing her back in her seat, I am sure she would have straddled the aisle as the plane landed.

"Please fasten your seat belts and put your trays in their upright position," requested the captain. "And ask the nice lady to sit back in her seat. She is giving her husband a heart attack."

The plane descended the last several miles of altitude by simply dropping straight down. I felt like one of those cliff divers from Mexico as earth came closer and closer. I could hear the screaming of the engines and the loud whistle of the wind through the wings.

As I sat in my chair gripping the arm rest and promising God that I would singlehandedly win every soul in the South, I felt an eruption in the middle of the plane. There was this horrible rumbling and a mighty rush of air across some opening in the plane. With a banshee scream, I informed everyone around us that we were going to die. The flight attendant seemed to disagree, thinking that the sound was just the landing gear being lowered.

"Can't the captain do that more quietly?" I inquired.

The attendant returned to her seat, and the pilot guided the plane onto the runway. With a small bump, then a forceful bounce, we rolled down the runway at monumental speed. The captain reversed the engines, and the plane slowed to a halt.

The plane taxied to a gate, and the passengers began to file out of the plane through the narrow aisle. As I departed the plane, the flight attendant handed me a brochure for Amtrak. I think that maybe she has a good idea.

An Exiting Note

I stood in the door to the kitchen and watched
as my tired wife fussed with the laundry,
separating them into whites and colors.
The soft bead of sweat trickled down her nose.

And as I watched, I thought,
Wouldn't it be grand to have clothes
that matched and blended
and never had to be sorted?

I stood at the door to the den and watched
as my wife tussled to repair my son's jeans
with tears across the knee.
While a lilt of hair hung across her eyes.

And as I watched, I thought,
Wouldn't it be grand to have clothes
that mended themselves
and never needed her touch?

I stood at the door to the kitchen and watched
as my wife pushed the iron,
pressing the shirt into submission,
a crinkled smile of fatigue on her face.

And as I watched, I thought,
Wouldn't it be grand to have
clothes that wrinkled into beauty
and never lost their luster?

I stood in the door to the great outdoors and watched
as God performed majestically.
He said to my heart, "I gave you such.
But you covered yours
with those rags."

Printed in the United Kingdom
by Lightning Source UK Ltd.
101253UKS00001B/424

9 781413 701784